A MUTUALLY BENEFICIAL PROPOSAL

The Unexpected Series Book One

HARPER REED

ISBN: 979-8832183060

Cover Credit—JoY Author Designs

Editor: Jamie Holmes

Dedication

To anyone who has ever cheated...
I hope the next bird that flies over you shits on your head.

Contents

Chapter 1   1
death by dong

Chapter 2   11
lickable strangers

Chapter 3   21
it's not you, it's me

Chapter 4   29
that motherfucker

Chapter 5   41
pain in my ass

Chapter 6   47
spill the tea

Chapter 7   55
look like a prostitute

Chapter 8   65
so much can be done with a tie

Chapter 9   77
push the boundaries

Chapter 10   89
better safe than itchy

Chapter 11   101
don't hide your pleasure

Chapter 12   109
fucking mint toothpaste

Chapter 13   121
all the dick love

Chapter 14   131
an even bigger fuckbag

Chapter 15   143
you make it so hard

Chapter 16   151
Okay Owen

Chapter 17   163
pee on you

Chapter 18   169
like a fucking angel

Chapter 19   181
a good dicking

Chapter 20   191
hotdog dick

Chapter 21   199
what the shit

Chapter 22   205
I'm ready

Chapter 23   207
not done

Chapter 24   213
a fucking goddess

Chapter 25   221
another dickass

Chapter 26   229
good fucking riddance

Chapter 27   241
jump off a bridge

Chapter 28   251
death was imminent

Chapter 29   259
lucky bastard

Epilogue   265

Connect with Me   275
About the Author   277
Also by Harper Reed   279
Now Available!   281
Preview   283

Chapter One

DEATH BY DONG

Ella

IF ANYONE EVER SAYS BURNING AN EX'S belongings in the backyard while a storm rages through town isn't cathartic, they're lying. Or maybe they've never been cheated on. Either way, this is my way of getting over Gavin Michaels, and I'm owning it.

With texts to my two best friends already sent, I stand under my covered patio, using the tiny firepit to burn every item Gavin left in my house before I kicked his ass out earlier.

The hurt I'd been feeling is still there, but the scorned woman in me is taking over while I do my best to scrub the images from my mind of him screwing someone else on my couch. Remembering what I walked in on after work makes me want to burn the sofa next, but I also don't want the neighbors to call the fire department.

Instead, I settle on making a mental note to ask Kenzie and Piper to help me carry the tarnished piece of furniture out to the front yard before they go home later. I'll tape a free sign to one of the cushions and pray it's gone by morning. Yep, that will have to work.

"Ella?" I hear Kenzie's voice inside my house above the crackling of embers from the shoes I just tossed in the flames.

"Back here," I call, hoping Piper is with her. I don't want to tell the story twice. Hell, I don't even want to say it once. Honestly, at this point in my life, my track record for keeping men is downright embarrassing.

Kenzie's fiery red hair appears first in my peripherals. She's wearing black yoga pants and a loose green top, meaning I interrupted her zen time. I momentarily feel bad but shake the feeling away. Moments like these are what friends are for.

Piper walks in right behind her and sits next to me. I take note of her adorable square-framed glasses and perfect messy bun of brunette hair. Tonight only serves to remind me how envious I am of her ability to only be in love with her career at a local publishing company. Though, she'll be leaving us sometime this year to go work at their new Los Angeles office, thanks to a promotion she received. As much as I'm going to miss her, I can't deny the happiness I feel for her, either.

"We got the SOS. What happened? Do you need an alibi? I can have one written out in ten minutes tops," she says, pulling out her phone to do just that. I let out a strangled chuckle.

"I kicked Gavin out, and I'm helping him get rid of the things he wasn't able to grab on his way out," I say, then toss a shirt next to the melting shoes.

Should I be worried about the smell of burnt plastic or the oddly colored flames? Probably. Am I? Not in the slightest.

"What did that fucker do?" Kenzie asks, taking the seat across from us.

I grunt. "Not what. *Who*."

"That cheese-dick bastard. I'm going to kill him." Kenzie is already red in the face on my behalf, and I love her for it, but there will be no murders taking place. He isn't worthy of our time. Once his things are gone, I'll force him out of my mind, too.

Just like the two relationships before him that ended in similar disaster. I'm beginning to think it's definitely me, and not them.

Piper reaches for me, offering a sweet smile. "I brought wine and chocolate."

I attempt to smile, because I'm more than thankful that she thought of reinforcements, but the action is near painful.

Kenzie stands and grabs some items from the pile I have in front of me. She tosses a pair of khaki shorts into the fire and lifts her upper lip. "He even dressed like a douche canoe."

I want to agree with her, but I can't. Gavin is hot.

Worse? He is all too aware of his prowess. His confidence is what drew me to him in the first place. I should have known better. Cocky isn't always best when it's coming from the mouth instead of between the legs.

"What about the vacation you already paid for?" Piper cringes even asking the question.

I had thought about that as soon as the initial shock wore off. I bought tickets for Gavin and me to go to an all-inclusive adults-only resort in Saint Lucia—ones that weren't cheap—and I'm having a hard time thinking about letting them go to waste.

"You two want to split the cost of a third ticket and come with me?" I ask, hoping to turn my romantic vacation into a girls' trip.

Piper considers my invite, but Kenzie immediately declines. "We have a blackout period at work these next two weeks. System upgrades, and they need all hands on deck, or so they say. I wish I could, if that helps."

It does, but I'm still bummed.

I turn to Piper, but the way she's counting on her fingertips doesn't bode well for me. "You're coming back when?"

"The seventeenth," I answer.

Piper kicks a pile of Gavin's shirts. "I can't. I need to be here on the fifteenth for my first editor's meeting. Unless you can change the return date? Though, that would cut your trip down from five full days to only three."

Hope springs inside me until I remember that Gavin

convinced me to be a cheap-ass and choose non-refundable or changeable tickets. Stupid cheating bastard. I never should have listened to him.

"We'd have to buy two new tickets home for the fifteenth." At this point, last-minute flights would probably cost my left tit.

Kenzie hands me a bottle of wine. Pink Moscato, my favorite when I'm not drinking hard alcohol. It's sugary, bubbly, and doesn't ever give me a hangover.

"You might want to take a drink before I tell you how much one-way tickets cost right now," she says.

"I don't even want to know. Maybe I just shouldn't go. What am I going to do by myself in Saint Lucia?" I groan, taking a long pull straight from the bottle. There will be no glasses for me tonight.

Kenzie waggles the brows above her hazel eyes. "Umm, I have several ideas, and one of them includes cabana boys. Sexy, unattached, tanned, and muscled cabana boys."

"I don't think your version of them is real. I'm sure it's more like middle-aged men in Hawaiian shirts serving the poor lonely women, then telling jokes about them when they return to their kitchen to fill more orders," I say.

It's been made painfully clear that I have no luck when it comes to men. Not even that time when I tried to have a one-night stand. Epic. Fucking. Fail.

I take several more gulps from the bottle. I'm

especially grateful for Piper when I see three more in the oversized bag she calls a purse.

The fire is burning through Gavin's belongings too quickly. I'm not sure what I'll do when I have nothing left of his to destroy.

I stare off into the darkness. I know I need to tell them the details of what happened. The quicker I do, the better I'll hopefully feel, but that doesn't make the words leaving my mouth any easier to get out.

"I got off work early today and didn't tell Gavin." I laugh darkly. "I thought I'd surprise him."

Piper and Kenzie wear matching frowns, but stay quiet, letting me get the words out in one go.

"When I opened the door, they were on the couch and naked and..." I shudder trying to finish the sentence.

"I didn't say anything at first. I only slammed the door. And the woman he brought into *my* house? Yeah, she merely smirked at me before digging her claws into Gavin's shoulders. The bastard scrambled up, sputtering on about how this wasn't what it looked like. Like I was supposed to believe that he'd been forced to put his junk in her stank."

"That fucking dick...ass," Piper mutters, making Kenzie and me burst into laughter. Something I very much needed.

"Dickass? That's a new one," Kenzie says.

Piper huffs. "Well, dick and asshole didn't seem like a good enough slur."

I reach a hand for hers. "Dickass is perfect."

"What happened next?" Kenzie asks.

"He threw clothes at her and helped her out the door while I tried to process what the hell I'd just walked in on. Once she was gone, he tried to apologize, but I threw a couch cushion at his head and told him to get the fuck out."

My stomach churns when I remember his still-hard dick standing proud for the woman he'd brought into the home we shared.

Piper raises a brow. "Did he actually leave?"

I shake my head. "He grabbed the rest of the clothes off the floor and ran for our room before I could think to rip his balls off. A missed opportunity I now regret. I went to the kitchen while he packed whatever shit of his he deemed important."

Kenzie's fists tighten in her lap. "And he just left without begging for your forgiveness?"

I shrug. "He passed by the kitchen on his way out. My close proximity to the knife drawer might have made him think twice about speaking to me so soon."

"That fucker," Kenzie mutters through gritted teeth.

Piper gives my arm a squeeze. "I know this is harder to accept than to say, but Gavin isn't worth any more of your time or heart after tonight. Try to remember that you're not alone just because he's gone, Ella."

My chest tightens painfully at her soft words. I know they're true, and that helps, but it doesn't take away the ache of having been cheated on. Again.

I should be a pro at going through the break-up

phases: shock, anger, grief, regret, more anger, and then acceptance.

Each one is more annoying than the last. At least until I'm able to get to acceptance. I just need to find a way to speed up the process, because spending weeks, possibly even months, moping over another failed relationship isn't something I want on my agenda.

Maybe some time alone being unable to avoid my feelings would get me there quicker.

I throw another shirt into the fire, watching the flames take on a blue hue from the colored cotton. Thunder cracks in the air. Summer storms are my favorite.

"I'm going to go on the vacation," I finally say.

Kenzie and Piper both snap their heads toward me.

"And fuck a cabana boy to get over the dickass?" Kenzie asks excitedly.

"Absolutely not. I'm swearing off men for a while. I'll be fine with the B.O.B.s in my life for the foreseeable future." Using a battery-operated boyfriend definitely isn't my first choice for pleasure, but it seems better for my mental health. At least until I can figure out how to *not* choose a cheating bastard for a boyfriend. Hell, one of them had even been my fiancé.

Blake Parsons. The thought of him still irks me.

"It's not a terrible idea. Maybe we can go to Suzy's before you leave and you can travel with a new B.O.B.," Kenzie suggests with a heavy wink, and I laugh.

"Yeah, I can see the TSA agents having loads of fun with a big dick in my bag showing up when they scan it through. That's a good time that I'm going to have to pass on. We'll go when I get back. Make a smut party out of it."

Kenzie still has an evil glint to her eye. "Oh, come on, El. It would be more embarrassing for them than you, I'm sure."

She's wrong about that. Maybe not if it was her dildo, but for me? I'd die of embarrassment right in the airport, causing myself even more shame from my grave when the internet found out. I can see the memes now: Death by Dong.

I shake the thoughts from my mind and throw the last pile of crap from Gavin on the fire. It's nearly full of ash, and the smell of materials I never should have burned is giving me a headache. Though, my heart feels better, and that was the main goal of my destruction.

"Who's ready to dance around in our underwear while we finish all the wine Piper brought, along with whatever we find in my cabinets?" I ask, hoping they won't mind the late evening on a weeknight.

I need my girls, at least for tonight. I want to avoid the grief stage until I'm already buckled in my seat on the plane. Otherwise, I might wuss out and stay home feeling sorry for myself when I need to remember how fucking awesome I am.

Kenzie and Piper share identical smiles that have one growing on my face as well. Yes, tonight will be amazing and Gavin will soon be forgotten, along with the two years I wasted on him.

I might be nearly thirty and alone, but I have the best girlfriends anyone could wish for. No matter how heartbroken I want to feel, I intend to move on toward grander and better things.

Gavin won't steal another minute of my life.

Chapter Two

LICKABLE STRANGERS

Ella

OH MY GOD, WHAT HAVE I DONE?

Kenzie and Piper dropped me off at the Charlotte terminals five minutes ago, but instead of going straight to security with my carry-on bag like I should have, I dart for the bathroom, trying to avoid hyperventilating in the largest airport in North Carolina.

Now, I'm staring in the mirror, trying to ignore the red blotches appearing on my normally sun-kissed skin or the section of wavy umber hair I missed earlier that morning when I was straightening the sometimes-unruly strands.

My green eyes look back at me, almost mockingly. I shouldn't go on this trip. I should take a taxi home and hide away for the next six days, but the harder I stare at myself, the stronger I try to feel. The waves of post break-up emotions are moving through me like a tsunami, and I refuse to drown.

"Fuck that. Fuck Gavin. Fuck the coffee stain on my new white shirt," I say, then I hear a giggle from the stall behind me.

Could this get any worse?

It absolutely could. I need to keep my thoughts positive and get through security before I officially chicken out.

I grab the handle of my suitcase, packed only with swimsuits, shorts, tank tops, sandals, and underwear. I didn't even bring makeup. I have no one to impress. Men will mean nothing to me while I'm gone.

I exit the bathroom, and a dark-haired man bumps into me, plowing through to security without even offering an apologetic glance back. He goes up to precheck like he owns the place.

"And this is further proof as to why I don't need a man in my life," I say to myself before heading toward the back of the long security line for those of us who didn't pay extra to skip steps.

Fifteen or twenty minutes later, I get to the front of the line, and the uniformed woman sighs at me. "Identification and boarding pass."

I hand over my passport and hold my phone with my flight information over the scanner. "You're not the name on the ticket, miss. You'll have to go check with the airline on your flight."

Shit. I scanned Gavin's ticket.

"I'm sorry. My phone was on…someone else's ticket. I have mine." I swipe on the screen and show her.

She grunts, clearly suspicious of me. "Scan it again."

I do as I'm told, worried she's about to tell me I can't go. Though, would that really be the worst thing? Probably not.

The longer I'm standing here, the more my stomach fills with concrete.

"Okay, go on through," she says and shoves my driver's license back at me.

I let out the breath I've been holding and move forward. I'm grateful my carry-on isn't heavy when I lift it onto the conveyor belt before putting my purse and tennis shoes into the provided plastic tub.

The next TSA agent doesn't appear to hate his job as much as the previous one when he guides me forward. I stand in the x-ray machine with my legs spread and arms up like I'm a criminal. The machine does its swoosh-y thing around me, then beeps, and I step out.

Another woman agent points at me. "Please, step to the side, ma'am."

I glance around in case there's anyone else she could possibly be speaking to. "Uh, why?"

"Random security check. You're the lucky winner this round. Please stand with your legs apart and hold your arms out to the side," she says.

This is incredibly embarrassing, but I comply, hoping it's over before too many people can gawk.

She begins at my ankles, checking my socks, then

moves to my shorts. She teeters a little from where she's kneeling, and her hands accidentally press a little too hard over my recently waxed and still-sensitive vagina. I make a noise not at all appropriate for the situation.

She raises her brow at me, and I shrug. "Normally, I get dinner before letting anyone get that close."

This agent cracks a smile and I realize this is as uncomfortable for her as it is me. She hurries to finish, only patting my boobs for a half-second.

I try to find some amusement in the feel-up, given I don't plan on it happening again anytime soon.

"Whose bag is this?" a man's voice booms over the crowd.

When I turn my head, a male agent is holding up— you guessed it—my carry-on.

I sigh and raise my hand once the woman is done searching me.

"Meet me at the counter, ma'am." He's fighting a grin, and something tells me I'm not going to like what he says next.

He sits my closed bag on the counter and leans over it, getting closer to me before he whispers, "Your *friend* set off a chemical alarm. I'm sure it's harmless, but we have to um, inspect it. Is there anything sharp in your suitcase I need to worry about?"

"My friend? What do you mean?" I ask. Even though I have no idea what he's talking about, dread is making me want to vomit.

He clears his throat, covering one side of his mouth

before whispering, "The toy you packed? The *adult* one."

"*The what?!*" I nearly shout, and heads turn my way.

I'm going to murder Kenzie. Literally fucking murder her. I don't care if she's been my best friend since fifth grade. She. Is. Dead. To. Me.

"We just have to swab it and make sure there's no threat in having it on the plane. Glycerin in certain items can trigger our machines from time-to-time," he says as if he's trying to make me feel better.

"Just throw it away. Please. I did not pack that."

His face turns serious, and he pulls my suitcase further away from me. "Did you leave your baggage unattended, ma'am?"

Great. Now he probably thinks the dildo is a mother-freaking bomb.

People are full-on gawking at me now, and I wish it was possible to die of embarrassment like I'd pictured when my traitorous best friend mentioned bringing a B.O.B.

I want this moment to be over more than my next breath. No, I *need* it to be.

"No. My best friend thinks she's funny and must have packed it for me before we left my house this morning. It's not dangerous, but I also don't want you to test it or leave it in my bag. Please, have mercy on me and throw the damn thing away."

I don't even know what dildo it is. Hell, it might not even be mine, but I don't care to even see the sex toy to find out. Mostly because if I can see it, then the people getting too curious around me will be able to as well. Nosy bastards.

"I still have to get it out of your bag and test it before you're allowed to board," he says, also noticing we've gathered a crowd.

I cover my face and mumble, "Just do what you have to and let me be on my way."

The zipper opens, and I keep my eyes closed. One person gasps a second later, then another laughs, followed by a whistle until another woman tells him to shut up.

Maybe she could be my new best friend. There's a vacancy in the spot currently.

My bag is closed, and the TSA agent shoves it closer to me. "I hope you have a good trip, ma'am."

I finally look at him again. He's grinning and no longer trying to hide his amusement at my expense.

My fingers grip the side handle of my bag, and I jerk it from the counter before heading to grab my purse and tennis shoes off the end of the conveyor belt.

I don't bother to stay in the security area to put my shoes on. Instead, I walk past several gates in only my socks until I find an empty section. Only then do I face the window and fall into the seat.

I want to laugh. I want to cry. I want to scream.

Though, I don't do any of those things. I robotically tie my shoes and take a deep breath before pulling my phone from my purse. I consider calling Kenzie, but I don't think I can handle her laughter right now. I send her a short text, instead.

Me: You're dead to me.

Then, I turn my phone on airplane mode and toss it back into the black hole of my purse. Serves her right to think I'm actually pissed at her. As much as I want to be, I know in a few weeks—or maybe months—I'll be laughing my ass off about this. Today just isn't that day.

I grab my stuff again and double check my gate number, along with how long I have until boarding. I have just enough time to grab a water and a muffin before they'll begin calling passengers.

Without any other issues, I get what I want and make it to my gate, only to see my name on the screen behind the counter for the airline.

I try and fail to stifle a groan when I begrudgingly make my way forward to find out what's happened now.

The young woman there smiles brightly at me with perfectly straight teeth and an adorable black bob cut I could never pull off. "How may I help you?"

"I'm Ella Danes," I say and point to the screen.

"Oh, yes. The previous plane we had scheduled is delayed, and we're using another to keep all other flights on track which means your seat changed. Let me print your new ticket so you know where to go."

And here I thought this trip couldn't get any worse. I'm probably going to be moved right next to the bathroom or in the back row. Lucky me. Saint Lucia better be worth all this hell.

"Here you go," the agent says, offering me another smile.

I wonder if she can smell the bad day on me.

"Thanks," I mutter and turn around while looking over the ticket. My eyes widen when I see it says 3A. I whip my head back. "Is this correct?"

She nods. "I hope you have a better day, Ella."

I don't know this woman, but I want to hug her. Hell, I could even kiss her. The only thing keeping me from doing so is the idea of her screaming and me missing my flight.

After everything I've been through this week and just today, first-class sounds like the perfect way to spend the next five hours.

My shoulders sag, and I meet her kind eyes. "You have no idea how much I needed this."

"We all need a reason to smile," she replies with a genuine grin.

Isn't that the truth.

I back up so she can do her job, then stand just tenor-so feet away from where people will line up. It's only another minute before first class is called, and I gladly hand the same agent my newly printed ticket.

She scans it and I thank her properly before heading toward the plane.

"Enjoy your flight," she replies.

I sure as hell plan on it.

I get to my seat, and I'm beyond giddy. Even though I have a good job in lending for a small-scale bank, making decent money that allows me to afford my house and car without worrying where my next meal will come from, I've never splurged on extras like this.

My bag gets shoved in the overhead compartment, but I keep my purse with me. I have my kindle inside and intend on reading during the flight. Well, so long as I can keep the motion sickness at bay.

As I'm situating my things, I take a moment to appreciate the lush leather seats and the way they hug my body. I also see the buttons for the recline option in case I want a nap. I'm not tired, but I might take one just for the hell of it.

The person next to me arrives. Low and behold, I'm nearly positive it's the guy who bumped into me earlier. I ignore him when he unbuttons his suit coat, loosens his tie, and takes his seat.

Okay, I try to ignore him, but he's rather attractive with his finger-length businessman haircut that's parted at the side, and the straight jawline, bright blue eyes, and... Oh, my God. What am I doing?

No. Men.

Not even vacation men. No matter what, I will stick to my period of celibacy while I focus on myself and my job and my friends and not the sexy man next to me.

"Hi," he says with a wave.

I raise my hand without saying anything. I'm afraid my words will betray me, just like my best friend did.

"Business or pleasure?" he asks.

If I say pleasure—which seems like a poor choice of

words on his part—and I'm alone, I'll look like a loser. If I say business and he asks what I do, I have no idea what to lie about, because I have no clue why a businessperson would come to Saint Lucia.

Instead of telling the truth, I say, "A little of both." Then, I turn on my kindle and hope he gets the point.

When he lets me start to read without further interruption, I think maybe he wasn't trying to be an asshole earlier when he brushed past me in such a hurry. Maybe he ate something bad the night before and couldn't wait to use the bathroom. Who knows?

Either way, I don't care. Or, more accurately, I can't care. I'm going to ignore the slight smattering of hair on his face, the way his nearly black hair glistens under the stream of sunlight coming through my window, and how I tighten my legs together. The more I glance at him, the more intrigued I am.

Son of a bitch. This cannot and will not happen.

The stranger buckles up and leans his head back. I silently sigh in relief that he doesn't try to continue the conversation.

I came on this vacation to heal and forget men. I want Saint Lucia to be the best damn vacation I've ever had, and I'm going to do whatever it takes to make sure that dream comes true.

No cabana boys for me. No lickable strangers. Only warm, sunny beaches and sugary drinks until I'm forced back to reality.

Chapter Three

IT'S NOT YOU, IT'S ME

Owen

MY BOSS IS THE NEEDIEST BASTARD ALIVE. I don't know why I still work for him, but I've been one of his executive assistants for too long now, and my patience for dealing with him is running thinner by the day.

After literally running from my taxi to get through security, I emailed him the week's itinerary for the third time. Now, I'm on the plane with no intention of connecting to the internet until we've landed. For the next five hours, I'm going to enjoy a little peace and quiet.

It's something I thought might not be possible with the intriguing woman sitting next to me, traveling alone and without a ring on her finger. Unfortunately, she seems keen on the book she's reading and not at all interested in conversation.

I peek over when she swipes the screen and grin when I read something about a hard cock and moaning. A dirty girl. Too bad she isn't friendlier.

While she's distracted with the words on the screen, I get a closer look at her. Her russet hair that falls past her shoulders and her lack of makeup is appealing. She glows with a natural beauty I'm normally not attracted to. In this case, it's hard for me not to continue my perusal, noticing her soft green eyes, plump lips, and toned legs sticking out from the jean shorts she's wearing.

I shift in my seat and lean my head back again. Maybe it would be better to work than sit here and get turned on by the knockout next to me.

The plane has already started to taxi, and once the all-clear from the flight attendants is announced, I'm the first one with my bag in hand. I unzip the leather case and catch her glance over.

She lets out a sigh. I can't tell if she's annoyed or something else, but I use that as my attempt to interact with her again.

"Not that you asked, but I'm headed to the island for business and have a few things to finish before I arrive. Hope you don't mind," I say, mostly sincerely.

Her response is more than I bargained for. Her eyes darken to emerald, a fire building in them from my mildly condescending tone. A fire I imagine any warm-blooded man would be up to the challenge of smothering, and I suddenly want that man to be me.

"It's a free country. You can do whatever you want." She tempers the smolder and shrugs.

Before I can respond again, a flight attendant comes along. "Drinks for the lovely couple?"

The siren next to me practically chokes. "We're *not* a couple, but yes, I'd love something sweet with vodka in it, please."

The attendant's fair skin becomes ghost-like. "My apologies. I'll get that drink for you, Miss. Anything for you, Sir?"

"Just a bottle of water, please and thank you."

She nods, a strand of blonde curls coming loose from her tight bun. When she turns around, I see a perfectly round ass underneath her blue skirt. Unfortunately, there's no attraction rising within me. No desire to slip her my number when she comes back.

No, my curiosity is stuck on the woman next to me.

Normally, I don't have trouble with the ladies, even with ones I hardly know. The fact that this one seems so resistant increases my intrigue.

When I turn back to her, the look of annoyance on her face has returned. She makes a sound from the back of her throat and stares at her kindle again.

Spiteful much? I think.

Someone must have pissed in her Cheerios before she left for the airport.

The attendant comes back with our drink choices, but this time I barely look up. My email has loaded, and I want to murder my boss.

Jack Harrington. CEO to Harrington Enterprises. A company that owns one of everything. Food chains, hotels, clothing stores, car dealerships. You name any sort of Fortune 500 business and it's almost guaranteed that Jack has dipped his toes into the venture.

He has no wife, no children, no commitments to anything other than his work, and he expects his employees to be the same way. I should have realized that earlier, considering he hired me on the spot when he saw me charming several women into giving me their numbers at the bar.

The red flags were all there, but when the job came with a six-figure salary, condo, and luxury car, it was easy to ignore everything else.

That was five years ago. At thirty-four, I'm a little wiser in my actions, but again, the job has a lot of potential benefits that I'd be walking away from if I quit now. One being the things I get when I'm not being Jack's bitch.

My job title is technically Executive Assistant, but, when the opportunities arise, I do so much more than just whatever my boss requests. My favorite being when I get to assist with group projects that help the struggling branches of Harrington Enterprises thrive again instead of getting shut down.

Secondly, one day, Jack will retire and, if I can stick with the company long enough, I might be able to make a difference in the world under the right leadership and put more of my talents to use.

In the meantime, I do my best to tolerate the barking orders I'm constantly getting.

The woman next to me snorts. The sound is adorable and endearing. I look over, and her hand is covering her mouth while her delectable body shakes.

"You know, if you're going to be such a distraction, you should share what's funny," I say with a wink.

Her head slowly tilts up, and her eyes meet mine. The fire is back in them, but she isn't as wound up as she was earlier. "I don't think you can handle what's in here." She waves the kindle.

I raise a brow and cock my head a little. "Are you sure about that?"

She drags her gaze from my eyes, over my wide shoulders, down my wrinkle-free custom suit and to my shiny dress shoes, then back up. The action takes maybe five seconds, but it is hot as fuck.

"Absolutely."

Her one-word answer makes me want to challenge her more, but I give up on that tactic.

I turn toward her in my seat. "I'm Owen Porter. If you share your name, I promise not to give you any other reasons to plot my murder for the rest of the flight."

Her tongue makes a clicking noise when she thinks before answering. "I'm sorry. It's not you, it's me."

I chuckle and relax back into my seat. "You know, I normally get a date or two before I hear that line."

She laughs and the sound is like soft bells to my ears. "Seriously. It's definitely me, but if you must know, my name is Ella Danes. Enjoy the rest of your flight, Owen."

Ella takes a sip of her cherry-red mixed drink before going back to her book.

My interest only piques after our brief interaction. What could possibly be wrong with her? She seemed very sure of her words, and I have little doubt they're true.

Though, I keep good on my promise and give my attention to the work on my laptop while trying and failing to ignore the sexy noises she makes while she reads next to me.

————

ELLA IS SLEEPING WHEN THE PLANE LANDS. NOT even the rough landing jolts her. I'm afraid if I touch her that she'll punch me, but I think she'd be more embarrassed to be sleeping there while everyone gets off the plane before her.

I take the chance and run my fingers over her forearm. Goosebumps rise on her sun-tanned skin, so I do it again. "Ella," I whisper, trying not to startle her.

"Hmm," she mumbles.

"It's time to wake up, Sleeping Beauty."

She leans toward me, and I freeze when her cheek rests against my shoulder.

After our earlier interaction, my instincts say she wouldn't be pleased about being so close to me. I unbuckle and turn to help position her against the window.

Her eyes don't even flutter from my movements, and I'm amazed by how deeply she's sleeping.

This time, I'm a little louder and firmer with my actions. "Ella, the plane landed."

My fingers wrap around her bicep, and I give her a solid shake.

Her left hand comes up, and I move my arm to block her. I don't know how I knew she was going to swing, but the fire inside her eyes earlier told me to tread with caution. Maybe I should thank my sister for all those hard-earned lessons during my childhood.

Ella's fist connects with my forearm, but the motion lacks conviction. Her eyes open and then widen. She covers her pink lips and mutters something I can't decipher.

I release her and grin. "What's that?"

Her fingers spread just millimeters apart. "I'm sorry."

"I'm just glad you weren't dead. Do you think you can make it off the plane on your own?" She nods. "Good. Welcome to Saint Lucia, Ella."

With those parting words, I grab my laptop bag and step into the aisle without giving her another glance. There's no need to get a final look when I'm hopeful I'll see her again. Preferably sooner rather than later.

Chapter Four

THAT MOTHERFUCKER

Ella

WHEN I STEP OUTSIDE OF THE AIRPORT WITH MY carry-on—sans dildo—my shoulders sag in relief. I made it through the worst part. I left North Carolina on my own. I survived the flight next to Mr. McHottie, a.k.a. Owen Porter. More importantly, I didn't have any drool on my face when he woke me up.

Now, I just need to find a taxi to get me to the hotel. There are limos and private cars in the first section of the departure area. I should have ordered one of those, but whatever. I'll splurge on dinner later tonight. I only have five full days to live it up and, if I'm being serious about getting over the-ex-who-shall-not-be-named, I'll have to step out of my comfort zones.

I walk further along the pathways and find the taxi line. Everyone is smiling and laughing, and not one person that I can see is alone. I try not to dwell on that, though. Being by myself isn't bad. Maybe this is exactly how things were supposed to work out.

The cynic in me is trying to combat my positive thoughts, but I do my best not to let the negative in. Instead, I remember the words Kenzie and Piper told me when they forced me out of the car earlier.

I am not the problem. I am not broken. I am enough.

My chest tightens when I say them to myself. The statements are easier to repeat than believe considering my last three serious relationships ended with the dickface men I let into my heart cheating on me.

What had I done wrong? Why wasn't I enough for them? Or what hadn't I done enough of?

"Fucking fuck," I mutter to myself with a shake of my head.

No. I didn't do anything wrong. Those piece-of-shit exes of mine did. I should have learned my lesson after nearly marrying Blake Parsons, but alas, it's taken two more heartbreaks to realize something has to change.

Blake was four years older than me. Mature, stable, attentive. Everything I could have asked for, hence the reason I'd told him yes when he proposed on our two-year anniversary. I chose a long engagement, waiting until the following spring to get married.

Maybe that was where I'd gone wrong. Though, Piper tells me it's where I went right, given she caught him at the bar with another woman, one he'd been in a relationship with for three fucking months.

I shudder and step into line for the taxis. Maybe I need to turn on my phone to call Kenzie and Piper. They're always good for reminding me not to think about the past. Well, at least the parts of it that bring me down.

I swipe the screen down to turn off airplane mode, and within seconds my phone is pinging with messages. I sigh, remembering the text I sent to Kenzie and expecting most of them to be from her.

Only they're not. They're from Gavin-the-cheater-Michaels.

I fucked up. Can't we just talk about this?

Come on Ella. Don't ice me out. You know we're good together.

Ha! I snort at that one. If we were so good together, the dickass wouldn't have brought another woman into *my* house.

You're being a little dramatic with this silent treatment. Let's be adults and talk about this.

He must have forgotten we were supposed to be on a flight together this morning. Or he didn't think I was capable of going without him. Hopefully, it's the latter.

It was one time. I swear it won't ever happen again. I was freaking out about the vacation. I overheard Piper and you on the phone. She asked if you thought I was going to propose. I'm not ready for that yet. Let's just pretend this never happened and move on.

That motherfucker.

Yeah, I'm going to pretend this never happened, but not just him cheating. The whole damn relationship. His messages only get worse, and I stop reading before blocking his number.

As hard as it is to believe some days, I need to remember that I deserve better. If that shit for brains freaked out over a fleeting comment from my best friend, then he isn't ever going to be the man I need in my life.

Right?

Damn it, I hate the doubts all these assholes have put in my head.

I'm almost to the front of the line for the taxis, and I check the messages from my friends. Kenzie of course never took my last text seriously. She replied with only inappropriate emojis followed by lots of hearts.

She's lucky I love her.

In our group chat, there are several motivational texts just for me, and I almost tear up while reading them.

Piper: You are going to have the best time because you are an amazing person, El.

Kenzie: Remember that this wasn't your fault. You deserve all the happiness.

Kenzie: PS—Fuck em all. Literally and figuratively.

Piper: Don't fuck them all. You'll come home with diseases, but don't be afraid to live, either. Do something you'd never have done before. Something just for you.

Kenzie: Piper is right. Sorta. Go show the world

the badass that is Ella Mother Fucking Danes. The one we already know and love.

"Ma'am, do you need a ride?" the man inside the taxi asks through the rolled-down window.

I swipe at my fresh tears and smile. "That would be great."

I give him the name of my resort and slide into the back seat of the white taxi car before responding to my friends.

Me: Thank you both for everything. I'm terrified right now, but it helps knowing you're both rooting for me to survive this week. I love you two so fucking much.

Piper: We love you too. Be safe.

Kenzie: All the love for you! Have fun!

I grin at their individual replies. Even if I never find my Prince Charming, I'll die a happy woman with these two as my best friends.

"What brings you to our lovely island?" the driver asks with an accent that's almost French-like, but not quite.

I look up to find dark but friendly eyes staring at me through the rearview mirror. He looks to be in his forties, and he either dyes his short ebony hair or has fantastic genes, because I don't see any grays.

"Vacation," I reply politely.

"By yourself?" he inquires.

I cringe, but then remember, if I'm really going to love who I am, I can't be embarrassed of my situation.

Gavin cheating isn't my fault.

"Yep. Thought it would be nice. Nobody to say no to things I might want to do," I say with a tilt of my chin.

He chuckles. "Smart woman. The Vistas has all the best adventures. You should be able to keep yourself quite busy if that's what you want."

My sigh is full of hope from his words. "That would be perfect."

"I recommend windsurfing. If you've never done it, you're in for a great time." His jovial smile tells me I should believe him, but the thought of trying something that adventurous... Well, it wasn't on the agenda before.

"I'll give it some thought," I reply, then turn to take in the sights around me.

The sky is crystal blue and there isn't a cloud to be seen above me. The sun is so bright that I can barely stand to stare up, even through my polarized sunglasses. I roll the window down and take a deep inhale. Salty ocean water coats my senses, and I sag in my seat.

Weekend trips to the beach are my favorite thing to do at home, and the scent of the sea brings me a sliver of peace I was afraid I wouldn't feel while here.

My driver points out his window. "There's your hotel."

My eyes widen. The pictures online hadn't done this place justice. The property sits atop a hill with sloping grass knolls, a golf course to the left, tennis courts to the right, and plenty of pathways between them leading to who-knows-where.

Immediately in front of the resort, separated only by the small road we were driving up, is the beach. The sand is nearly white, and the water is as clear as the skies above.

Cabanas are lined up, and people everywhere are laughing and having fun. There even a couple of volleyball games going, bringing me back to my high school days. I used to have a blast playing. Maybe I could reignite that passion during my trip.

The taxi turns into the resort. Large light-tan marble columns with white swirls are holding up the massive overhang to the entry. Staff dressed in matching white polos and khaki shorts are waiting with bright smiles.

When the driver comes to a full stop, my door is opened.

"Welcome to The Vistas, Ella. My name is Rosa. I'll be available for the entirety of your trip, making sure everything is as you wish. How was your flight?" the young woman asks me, her accent matching that of the taxi driver, and I realize, from my earlier research of Saint Lucia, it's Creole, not French.

I blink rapidly, staring at her round face, wide chocolate eyes, and umber skin. "How do you know my name?"

She winks. "That's part of my job. Let me take your bag and you can tell me all about your flight while we head to your room. I've already completed your check-in process."

Rosa hurries along, her short dark-brunette hair

bobbing as she does. She turns back when she realizes I haven't followed. "Are you coming, Ella?"

"Uh, yeah. I just need to pay for my ride." I reach into my purse and grab my credit card.

The driver takes the plastic from me, and I stay leaning against the window until he's finished. I notice a picture of two young kids and a woman between them that I assume to be his wife. The sight of his lovely family causes a pang of jealousy to spark within me, but I shake the nonsense away when he hands my card back.

"Don't forget to try windsurfing. It's not every day you get to visit the world's best island." He smiles again before putting the car back into drive.

I nod and step away. Rosa is waiting for me and still too happy for someone in the service industry. Her grin is highlighted by her smooth dark skin, and I instantly want to like her.

"All set?" she asks, and I nod. "Great! Let's get you settled, then."

We walk through the front, and I notice there are no doors on any of the exits. Everything is open, and fresh air is carried through the opulent room by a light breeze.

Marble floors that match the columns from outside span as far as I can see. The ceiling is vaulted and covered in white oak slats. There is a concierge area, but Rosa bypasses that and heads for the bank of elevators.

"After you." She gestures right when the shiny black doors open.

I step inside to find the interior covered in what I

assume to be stainless steel and an electronic screen with four unmarked buttons beneath it. Rosa presses one and then scans a card before turning toward me.

"So, your flight. I hope it was well," she says.

I nod. "It was actually great once I got on the plane. I was upgraded to first class."

Rosa whistles. "Lucky you. Let's see if I can match the airline's kindness with some of the adventures that we have planned for you. I've adjusted your itinerary given the changes in guests. Personally, I think it's even better than before."

"Excuse me?" Confusion chokes me for several reasons. The first being how in-the-know Rosa seems to be. She knew my name and knows Gavin didn't come with me, even though I never told the resort. The second confusion being that I never signed up to have this kind of service. I only chose this place because they had the most activities included with the all-inclusive booking.

While the price was higher than the others I looked at, I certainly didn't think I had selected the fanciest of hotels, either.

"I'm sorry, Ella. Let me start over. My name is Rosa. I'm your personal concierge that has been included in your stay. I knew who you were because you were required to upload your passport before we confirmed your booking, which means we have your picture on file. We have connections with the airlines to make sure our guests catch their flights. When I saw Mr. Michaels didn't join you, I took it upon myself to adjust the plans I made for you in hopes of making things less troublesome for you. I see now that I've made things worse, and I apologize. If you would like someone else to be assigned to assist you, I will let my manager know."

Rosa's speech makes me feel like an asshole. Of course, they had my picture. Though, it seems unconventional for the hotel to track their guests, the gesture, while creepy, is appreciated.

"It's okay, Rosa. I was just surprised. I didn't pay much for this room and I didn't expect all of this. You've gone above and beyond, and I've only been here five minutes."

Her face brightens. "We've had some changes in management, and they've made The Vistas even more magical. Don't worry, there won't be any hidden extra charges when you check out."

Maybe luck is finally in my corner. First-class upgrade on the flight and now this? I'm not sure if I want to cry or jump up and down like a child.

The elevator stops, and the doors swoosh open. The hallway is wide, and there's a sign for rooms 1501-1519 on the right and 1520-1539 on the left.

"Right this way, Ella," Rosa says and steps out first.

The walls are covered in light-blue paint with white trim in the middle, breaking up the monotony. The runner beneath my feet covering the now familiar marble is plush and a light gray.

"What room am I in?" I ask.

"1539. Corner room with a great view if I do say so

myself," she answers, pulling my bag behind her like she couldn't fathom doing anything else more joyous.

Less than a minute later, we arrive at my door. Rosa pulls out the same card she used in the elevator and swipes it over the black square on the door. It beeps and pops open.

"Welcome to your home away from home at The Vistas, Ms. Danes," Rosa says, stepping back to let me in first.

I enter the room, and it's twice the size of normal hotels I've stayed at. Two walls are covered in tinted windows with curtains tucked into the corners. The bed is opposite to the windows and closer to the soft yellow walls that have a few abstract art pieces gracing them.

Rosa's bright smile grows. "The bathroom is over here. The jetted tub is to die for."

I'm beginning to realize that everything here is to die for. For the first time since I caught Gavin with that woman on my couch, I start to believe that just maybe everything is going to be okay.

Chapter Five

PAIN IN MY ASS

Owen

MY ROOM IS ON THE TWENTIETH FLOOR AND
three doors down from my boss, which I'm not terribly
excited about, but at least the view of the rolling ocean
and white beaches is something right out of a magazine.

I have a balcony outside my bedroom, and I've
decided it just might be my favorite spot—as long as I
don't get too close to the edge.

The sound of waves below lulls me into the
beginning stages of relaxation, and I try not to think
about all the things I'm going to be forced to do while
I'm here. The mixer tonight to officially welcome
everyone to the island, the outdoor activities tomorrow,
bullshit team-building events later on, and whatever else
will undoubtedly come up.

I wish Jack would call this what it is: a trip to make

his dick feel bigger. Every senior employee will be throwing themselves at our CEO and begging to be noticed. If only they knew what working too closely to Jack really entails.

A knock on my door has me turning around to head back inside. My assigned concierge Robert is on the other side and enters with the drink cart I ordered. If I'm expected to survive the coming days, it's not likely I'll be able to do it completely sober.

"Here are the items you requested, Mr. Porter. Is there anything else I can get you?" he asks. Robert's older, maybe in his fifties with charcoal-gray hair and dark-blue eyes that wrinkle at the sides when he smiles.

I shake my head. "I'll call if I need anything else."

Robert exits the room quietly, and I make myself a whiskey sour. Just when the glass touches my lips, my phone vibrates.

I glance at the screen and groan before I answer. "Hello, Mr. Harrington."

"Quit with that bullshit, Owen. We're not in the boardroom. You know to call me Jack." His voice booms, and I have to pull the phone away from my ear before putting it on speaker and setting it down.

"Right. Jack. What can I do for you?" I ask, annoyed he hasn't even let me unpack before needing something else. He might want me to address him by his first name, but he's not calling to chat like old friends.

"I need you to go downstairs and grab the paperwork that just came through for me," he demands.

I shake my head. The hotel staff could just as easily complete this task. Some days, I swear he gets off on seeing how much he can annoy me with the most menial of requests.

"Of course. I'll head down right now," I reply instead of saying what I really want to.

"That's my boy. I'll see you soon."

Jack hangs up without another word and I chug my whiskey sour, glaring at the phone that I wish I could throw into the ocean. The drink burns as it travels down my throat and helps calm my rising emotions. I need to figure out what I'm willing to continue sacrificing, because my disdain for this job only continues to grow.

I've already taken off my tie and suit coat, which means I'm not exactly dressed to see my boss, but I'm out of fucks to give in the moment. I pass by both items that I tossed on the couch not ten minutes earlier and head for the door. My hands pat my pockets to double-check I have my keycard before I let the door close behind me.

The elevator is around the corner and already waiting for me. That fact feels almost mocking, like the damn machine knows I'm running bitch errands.

I step inside, scan my card, and press the lobby button when the screen flashes with my choices. Soft music hums in the background, and I rock back and forth on my feet until the doors slowly open to the ground floor.

The fresh ocean air greets me, and I take a deep inhale before stepping out. I need to remember that I'm going to have free time at some point, and there will be benefits to being on this work trip. It won't all be a pain in my ass.

I walk toward the concierge counter, and I see Robert. He smiles brightly when our gazes meet.

"How can I help you, Mr. Porter?" he asks when I approach.

My fingers drum on the smooth granite counter. "First, you can call me Owen. Secondly, I'm supposed to be picking up some papers that were printed for Jack Harrington in Room 2001."

Robert moves to the cabinets behind him and searches for a good thirty seconds. I internally groan, not wanting to deal with Jack if the papers aren't here as he expects.

"I'm sorry, Mr. Por—Owen, but I don't see any documents," Robert says apologetically.

My phone dings with a text.

Jack Harrington: Looks like someone else brought them up. Never mind.

Asshole doesn't even say, "Sorry for the inconvenience."

I send back a thumbs up that I wish is the middle-finger emoji.

"That's okay. Apparently, the papers have already been delivered. Thanks for looking." I turn to head back to my room.

"Would you like me to book something for you? I have a list of options I prepared that won't conflict with the schedule of your work functions," Robert says before I've even made it three steps.

I sigh and swivel back around with a polite smile. I don't want to be rude. "Can I take the list with me and get back to you?"

He nods. "Of course. Let me grab that for you."

Robert pulls a folder from underneath the counter. There are several brochures and papers, but he only pulls out one, sliding it across to me.

I raise the paper up a little before folding and tucking it into my back pocket. "Thanks for this."

"It's my absolute pleasure, Owen."

When I'm halfway to the elevator, the sight of someone familiar catches my attention and I stop. Walking toward the coffee bar is Ella, the woman from the plane. She's changed from her jean shorts to a light-pink bikini with one of those sheer cover-up dresses that falls to her mid-thigh.

Her thick brown hair is piled atop her head, and loose strands frame her oval face. I consider waiting for her to feel me staring, but I can't stop myself from impatiently taking a step forward. Though, when I begin walking in her direction, I see subtle changes coming over her.

Her eyes pinch, then widen. Her lips flatten into a thin line, and her hands are twisting together in front of her while she slows her pace.

A man about my age in gray swim trunks and a white

tank top is standing with a blonde woman in a black bikini that leaves little to the imagination.

The man is smiling and waves at Ella. She doesn't retreat, even though her face is paling, and she isn't returning this man's enthusiasm about seeing each other.

The woman drapes herself over the guy and splays her hand over his chest, revealing a massive diamond on her ring finger.

I'm close enough now that I see how Ella gulps and lowers her gaze. Whoever these people are, they aren't her friends.

I'm driven to help her, but I have no idea why. Maybe because she seemed a little broken on the airplane, or because she had no interest in me, or merely because the sight of her makes my dick twitch. Whatever the reason, I'm either about to piss her the hell off and get slapped in the face, or I'm going to save her from whatever dreadful situation she's suddenly found herself in.

Chapter Six

SPILL THE TEA

Ella

AFTER UNPACKING MY STUFF, I DECIDE TO GO for a swim and let the sun take away my stresses. I put on my favorite pink bikini with my sheer black cover-up. Enough of my curvy ass is concealed that I feel comfortable walking through the hotel to the pool.

At the last minute, I decide some caffeine will be helpful since I was up before the sun to catch my flight. My unexpected nap on the plane only made me drowsier. Except, when I'm within twenty feet of the coffee bar, I want to die.

How can life be so cruel? What did I do to deserve its wrath?

I need to turn around and run as far from this place as possible, but it's too late. Blake saw me first. If I flee,

I'll only look like a fool, and that's the last thing I can handle right now.

With one forced step after another, I close the distance between myself, my ex-fiancé, and his new whatever.

She's tall and thin and perfect, and there isn't a piece of her that's left a mystery to the guests of the resort. A surge of jealousy races through me, and I'm reminded how much I loved Blake and how badly he hurt me when I learned he was cheating.

Looking at him now, six years later, he's even more handsome than I remember and is grinning at me as if we're long-lost friends. I don't know how I'm going to act, but I have no time to prepare for whatever is about to happen.

"Ella Danes? What a surprise," Blake says.

"Who's this, baby?' the woman coos, lifting her arm and drumming her fingers over his muscled chest. The action brings attention to the shining rock on her left hand. A vice closes around my chest, and I can't speak.

"This is...an old friend. Ella, this is my wife Cammie. We're on our honeymoon." The way he ends the sentence tells me he expects me to reply with my reason for being in Saint Lucia, but I have nothing good to say.

Instead, I blink like a dumbass. I'm frozen. My eyes can't leave the ring on Cammie's hand. I can't even breathe. The only thing that could have made this worse was if he was here with the woman that he cheated on me with.

"Are you okay, Ella?" Blake says, leaning forward and waving his hand in front of my face.

"There you are, beautiful," a man says from behind me right before he wraps his hands around my waist, squeezing tight.

I flinch at the contact, but the shock I'm experiencing from seeing Blake and hearing he's married prevents me from punching the stranger in his balls. He moves to stand beside me, leaving an arm wrapped around my waist and fingers gripping my hip possessively. With his free hand, he reaches for Blake.

"I'm Owen Porter. Ella's lucky lover."

I choke on air and try to push him away. I finally recognize him as the man from the plane. What in the actual fuck is happening right now?

"Oh, sweetheart. Don't be ashamed. At least I didn't say f—" Owen says, but I cut him off with a glare before he can finish the sentence. I have no idea what he was going to say, but lover was bad enough.

"Fiancé? Are the two of you here celebrating your engagement?" Cammie asks excitedly, dropping her hand from Blake, whose jaw is now tense.

Owen's grin spreads and he nods. "We are. Might even consider getting married on the beach while we're here. I just can't get enough of this one. I want to make sure she's mine before anyone else can think to steal her from me."

I'm fully aware that every word spewing from Owen's mouth is false, but I can't lie. He is turning this incredibly uncomfortable situation into something I can walk away from with my head held high.

Blake's eyes meet mine, dark and accusing, as if I'd been the one to ruin our past relationship. "No long engagement?"

I don't let his change in demeanor get to me, and I smirk at him, hoping my gaze conveys all the hate I feel for the cheating bastard. "Didn't quite work out so well for me last time. Or maybe it saved me from ruining the rest of my life. Either way, Owen has made me a new woman. He really knows what he's doing when it comes to *all* aspects of a relationship."

Blake makes a rough sound from his throat and takes a step back. Owen is glancing between the two of us, hopefully not reading too much between the lines, and Cammie just seems clueless of the awkward situation.

She giggles. "Girl, you're making me jealous. I can feel the heat coming off the two of you in waves."

Blake pulls his wife closer. "Well, then. I'm happy for you, Ella. We should all do dinner. We're here for the week."

I want to laugh in his face. There isn't a scenario in this world that would ever make me agree to dinner with that cheating bastard.

"Oh yes. I hardly ever meet Blake's friends. I'd love to get to know you, Ella," Cammie says, and I instantly feel bad for her. If Blake's keeping her a secret from his friends, that doesn't bode well for him being faithful.

Owen slides his arm around me again, and this time I

burrow closer to him. "We'll see if we can clear our schedule and be in touch," he says.

"No hard feelings if we can't get anything to line up." Blake's fake smile and stiff nod make my grip on Owen tighten more than is appropriate, given I don't know him.

Blake drags Cammie away from us, and I let out a shuddering breath. Owen's fingers rub over my hipbone, and I try to step away, but his lips are on my ear in the next second.

"He's still watching," Owen whispers.

Damn this man for being so observant.

A few more moments pass before Owen loosens his hold. "So, who was that guy?"

"None of your business," I reply while pretending I don't find the smattering of hair on his chest sexy as hell that I can see from the undone buttons of his dress shirt.

Owen's gaze lowers to mine. "On the contrary, Ella. I just saved you. I think I get to know why it was necessary. Answering my question is the least you can do in return."

He makes a valid point, one I don't really like, but I'm not a bitch. I can answer the question.

"His name is Blake Parsons. We were engaged for a short time about six years ago," I say, hoping that's enough to placate the stranger. I'm trying not to notice that he looks even better when he's dressed down. On the airplane, he looked too uptight, but this relaxed version of him is...

I give my mind a mental shake. Nope. Not going there.

"Why didn't you get married?" Owen asks, reaching for a coffee cup while waiting for the response I don't want to give.

It's a simple question, but that doesn't make the answer any easier to share. Plus, I don't know this guy. I don't need to explain my past when I didn't ask for his help. He intervened all on his own.

"It doesn't matter why. I appreciate your help, but they're gone now. I'd like to get my coffee and go find a place to lay under the sun where I won't be interrupted," I say as nicely as I can while joining him at the counter.

Owen's light-blue eyes peer into mine. He's searching for something I hope he doesn't find. I came here to forget men. Not to find myself a vacation fuck-buddy. My increasing libido gets no say in the matter.

The determination rolling off Owen isn't boding well for me, but he finally concedes and pulls his now full cup out from under the fancy machine spout. "Okay, Ella Danes. You enjoy the sunshine. Should you need my services again, given we're now engaged, I'm in Room 2007."

I smile because it seems like the polite thing to do instead of ogling him or flat out ignoring his words like I probably should do. "Thank you, Owen Porter. I'm sure that won't be necessary, though."

He tsks, the sound dripping in disappointment. "We'll see."

I watch him walk away, shamelessly checking him out and appreciating the way his charcoal slacks shape his ass. Yeah, I need to stay far away from that man. He's trouble with a capital T.

Yet, the rising smile on my face is all thanks to him and the fact that he saved me from making an idiot of myself in front of Blake and his new wife.

I don't know how Owen knew to interfere, or why, but I tell myself that neither of those things matter.

I get myself a Frappuccino from the golden contraption and reach for my phone that I have tucked into the corner of my swimsuit top.

There's a message from Kenzie asking for an update on the trip, but instead of replying via text, I hit the video chat button and walk out the nearest exit with the needed caffeine in my other hand.

I'm mid-sip when her beautiful face appears on the screen. "That looks yummy," she says.

"It is. Along with the view." I reach my thumb over and flip the camera.

Blue skies, the pool, and palm trees grace the screen. "You lucky bitch."

I click the button again so Kenzie can see me. "Ha! I don't know about that. You'll never believe who I just ran into."

She frowns. "Who?"

I glance around me before answering. "Blake fucking Parsons and his shiny new wife."

"You've got to be shitting me. Please tell me he didn't have the balls to talk to you."

I grimace. "He did, and I had no choice but to participate in the conversation."

"Damn, I'm so sorry, El. I wish we were there with you. I would have punched that fucker in the throat. That had to be the most uncomfortable situation ever."

Walking in on my boyfriend screwing another woman was worse, but I don't need to say that out loud.

"It certainly wasn't enjoyable, but I did have some help," I say.

Kenzie points at the screen with raised brows and a smirk. "Girl, you're blushing. You better spill the tea and tell me what happened."

"Well, there was this guy from the plane that I didn't tell you guys about in my earlier text."

Her eyes brighten, and her grin grows. "Go on."

Chapter Seven

LOOK LIKE A PROSTITUTE

Owen

ELLA DANES. I DON'T KNOW WHO SHE IS, BUT everything inside me says she's different. Her passionate eyes, the soft but pointed edges of her personality I've witnessed so far, and the underlying feeling that there are parts of her begging to be discovered by the right person.

After the interaction with her ex, I know she's been hurt, but her insistence on staying away from me further intrigues me. Though, I'm not supposed to be in Saint Lucia looking for a fling. I'm here to work and, with any luck, to find some time to unplug from the chaos that makes up my world.

Except, even as I'm sitting on my balcony, I can't get Ella out of my mind. I also can't stop myself from searching for her below, even when it makes my stomach churn to look down.

Being on the twentieth floor, I barely see her, but that's enough to keep me distracted. She's removed the sheer dress and is currently laying on one of the loungers, holding something in her hands. Maybe she's reading again, maybe she's browsing apps, or maybe she's on the phone.

The fact that I spend a full five fucking minutes trying to figure which it could be is enough to drive me mad.

I return to the inside of my room and grab the list Robert gave me. I didn't actually intend to call him about any of the activities, but I need a distraction that doesn't make me feel like a damn stalker.

There's windsurfing, jet skis, whale watching, hiking, golfing, and plenty of other things, but most of them I don't have time for today. There's less than two hours before the evening event starts, so I choose to go jogging on the trails.

I change out of my business clothes and into workout shorts with tennis shoes. I drop my phone into the right pocket of the shorts and slip my room key into the other one before grabbing a bottle of water from the fridge and heading out of my room. When I get to the elevator, Jack is there. He's in a full suit with a bright red tie standing out over his chest and protruding stomach.

I force a smile to my face. "Hello, Jack."

Russet eyes that match his dyed, slicked-back hair appraise my unclothed chest with disdain. "Are you headed out like that?"

"Just going for a quick run before the mixer tonight. I promise to be fully dressed when I arrive." With practiced effort, I manage to keep the irritation out of my tone when I answer.

"Of course you will be. I'd expect nothing less from you. You're one of my best employees. About tonight, though. I need you to go with Natalie. She's been a bit of a problem lately and I need some help keeping her happy, if you know what I mean."

Yeah, not fucking happening. Not because I don't like Natalie. I consider her a friend, and I don't have too many of those within Harrington Enterprises, but the last time I let Jack pick my date, it came with strings attached that I wasn't fond of.

Though, I can't deny my curiosity that Natalie could possibly be considered a problem. She doesn't usually speak unless spoken to and always gets her work done. I did hear she was recently promoted to Head of Accounting, which was an announcement that came out of nowhere. I now assume it has something to do with Jack thinking Natalie is a problem to be dealt with.

I want to help her, given how vicious I know Jack can be, but I also don't want to be directly involved. Maybe I can chat with her tonight without Jack knowing.

"I already have a date for the evening. Maybe I can take Natalie out another night this week," I say, silently hoping that will be enough to placate my boss.

Jack grins. "Already picking up the ladies? Of course, you are. Not a problem. I'll make sure someone else takes care of Natalie for the night. If we're lucky, maybe they'll solve all my problems tonight."

I don't know how to respond without showing my disgust for the man next to me. I manage to keep my words short and simple. "Thanks for understanding, Jack."

We part ways, and I'm tempted to reach out to Natalie right then, but this seems like a conversation better had in person.

I also need to find a date for tonight, and I know just the person to ask. Ella Danes now owes me a favor, and I have no shame in asking for payment.

———

ALMOST AN HOUR LATER, I'M COVERED IN SWEAT and breathing hard. After running more than I intended to, thanks to a wrong turn on the trails, I make my way to the pool, hoping Ella is still there.

I should have gone to her first, but I thought I'd be back sooner and wanted to spend my run concocting a plan that Ella couldn't say no to. It's probably a terrible idea to mix business with pleasure, but I can't stop myself from attempting to make this come to fruition.

She hasn't been far from my mind since getting off the airplane. If she outright turns me down, I'll figure something else out. I saw the hurt in her eyes when she'd been forced to speak with Blake. I don't want to be another asshole she has to deal with or the one who taints her vacation.

If anything, I want to be the one who makes this a trip she can never forget, because something tells me that this particular woman deserves more than a little happiness in her life.

Luck happens to be on my side today. Ella is still camped out next to the pool. Her hair is now wet and fanned out behind her, and she's laying comfortably on one of the loungers.

My eyes zero in on her pebbled nipples, and my dick wakes at the sight of her.

Stand down, boy. We can't come on too strong with this one.

He doesn't listen, and I'm forced to adjust myself before I get to her chair. I can't let her notice my physical interest before I've had the chance to say what I need to.

"Ella," I say softly since her eyes are closed.

She flinches and stares up at me with a hand covering her chest. "Mother shit. Don't do that."

I smirk. "What? Don't say your name?"

She glares, shaking her head while sitting up and I hear the click of her tongue again. I wonder if she realizes when she makes the noise.

"I meant don't sneak up on me, jerk." She reaches for her towel and squeezes the ends of her hair that are dripping with water now that she's sitting up.

I kneel so we're eye level. "I do like your choice of

words, though. Mother shit is a new combination I haven't heard."

"Did you need something, Owen?" she asks with exasperation in her tone.

And here goes nothing.

"In fact, I do. I'm calling in the favor you owe me."

She laughs in my face. "I did not agree to return any favors to you. What you did earlier was all on you."

"The way you willingly nestled against my body said otherwise," I counter and smirk.

Her legs swing off the chair, and I'm nearly kicked in the face. "Listen, Owen. I've had a shitty fucking week, and I don't need you to make it worse. I appreciate what you did with Blake earlier, but I didn't ask for that. I don't want to swap favors. I can pay you if you want, but money is all you're getting out of me."

I scoff. "Do I look like a prostitute to you?"

The heat in her eyes makes me desperate for her answer, but one never comes. She only continues to glower at me.

"Okay, in all seriousness, I need your help. I don't want to bother you or ruin your vacation. In fact, I only want to make it better, and I feel like this proposal can be a win-win for both of us."

Ella gulps hard. "You want to *actually* propose?"

The panic in her voice makes me almost feel sorry for her, but I have an inkling that she wouldn't want pity from me.

"Wrong choice in words. I have a proposition for you," I say.

She raises a brow, and one side of her plump lips raises. "I'm not sure that's any better, Owen."

"Some would disagree, but let's not get off topic here. At least one of us is bound to run into that ex of yours. Do you really want to be alone every time you see him or chance him seeing me with another woman that I will undoubtedly be forced to have as a date for my work function if you don't agree to help me?"

Ella bites her lip while contemplating what I said. I don't know anything about this Blake guy, but I can already tell she doesn't want to be made a fool in front of him. I hate taking advantage of her when she seems so fragile already, but I truly believe this can be a mutually beneficial proposal.

Her light-green eyes stare at me, likely calculating whether she can trust me or not. "Why me? You don't even know me."

I place my hand over hers and ignore the way she stiffens from my touch. "Because you, Ella Danes, seem like a good person, and there aren't too many of us left in this world. We have to stick together when we can. I'm not looking to take advantage of you. I'm trying to avoid my boss getting me involved in whatever he's got going on and expecting me to be someone I'm not anymore."

Her gaze lowers at me. "Not anymore? What does that mean?"

I want to lie to her and tell her that's not what I

meant, but something inside me says to be honest even if it makes me sound like an asshole.

"My boss hired me because he was impressed with the way I could get the number of any woman at the bar, even if they'd just seen me hitting on another. He said he wanted someone at his side who wouldn't blink at hurting another when he had something to gain. After working for Jack Harrington for the last five years, I've begun to see the man he wanted me to be isn't one I can be proud of."

"Then, why do you still work for him?" she asks.

"That's a very valid question that you can have the answer to if you agree to my proposition. For now, let's just say I'm working to rectify that, but until I do, I could use your help to keep me out of whatever Jack has going on. Plus, while you're hanging out with me, I'm happy to show Blake what he's lost, if that would make you feel better."

I see the tension rising in her shoulders, and I'm worried I've gone too far with my request, but there's a softening in her eyes that says I haven't completely lost. It doesn't allow me to shut up and wait for her response.

"There's a welcome mixer I'd like for you to join me at tonight. Be my date and decide about the rest of the week after the night is over." I glance at my watch, then grimace. "Oh, and the party starts at six."

She leans over and checks the time as well. "You need me to be presentable for a social event in under thirty minutes?"

I shrug. "As long as you brought a dress with you, then all you have to do is brush your hair and slip it on, right?"

Ella shakes her head. "You're such a man."

She hasn't told me no, which I'm taking as a yes. "What if I buy you a dress?"

Her answering laughter raises my hope that she's going to agree and also makes me want to kiss her senseless.

"You're going to make me feel like Vivian Ward. You can't buy me a dress," she answers.

"I'm not asking you to sleep in my hotel room for the week, Ella," I point out.

The widening of her eyes tells me she's surprised I'm familiar with *Pretty Woman*, but we don't have time to dwell on my movie knowledge.

"All I'm asking for is tonight, Ella. We'll drink and have some fun. That's it," I add, begging her not only with my words, but with my lowering lip.

She sighs and fights a smile. "Just tonight?"

I nod, then glance at the time again and cringe. "There are only twenty-four minutes left now."

She huffs and grabs her cover-up. "I don't know why I'm doing this. This is going to be horrible. I should say no."

I chuckle. "Are you talking to me or yourself?"

She shoots me a glare that makes me put my hands up in surrender.

"I want a dress at my door in ten minutes or less. Any later and you can find yourself another Vivian."

Ella is out of her chair and ten feet away from me before I stand. I watch her ass bounce while she storms off. My teeth click together at the thought of biting her perfectly round rear end.

Unfortunately, I don't have time to fantasize. I race behind her to find Robert. If I'm going to pull this off, I'll need his help.

Chapter Eight

SO MUCH CAN BE DONE WITH A TIE

Ella

WHAT THE FUCK AM I DOING?

I can't answer that question, because if I think too hard on what I've agreed to then I'll have to declare myself insane. Yes, Owen helped me out when I was floundering in front of Blake and his new wife, but I didn't ask for that. His actions also didn't mean I owed him anything.

Yet, when I nearly lost myself in his cobalt eyes, I couldn't stop myself from feeling obligated to help him as well.

His boss sounds like an ass for expecting his employees to have dates for work functions—especially out-of-town ones—but that's not something I want to concern myself with. I've said yes to Owen and need to make myself presentable enough to attend a corporate mixer within the extremely limited timeframe he's given me.

There's a chance Owen won't get me the dress on time and I can get out of this whole insane situation. Except something about the desperation in his pleas tells me that he'll deliver the outfit in plenty of time. Plus, his confidence makes me believe he's good at everything he does, like procuring clothes and...nope. I'm not going there.

I remind myself that I'm merely helping this man with a difficult situation like he did for me. After that, I never have to speak to him again. Owen said he really only needs me for tonight. The event couldn't be *that* intolerable. Right?

I dial Rosa from my room since I didn't see her when I sped through the hotel, and she answers on the first ring. "How can I help you, Ms. Danes?"

"I need a curling iron and makeup within the next ten minutes. I might be in the shower, so just come on in," I say, because something tells me she'll be in my room within five minutes.

"See you soon," she replies before ending the call.

I'm stripped out of my swimsuit before I reach the shower and jump in without waiting for the water to warm. Time is not on my side here.

I rinse and have conditioner in my hair within seconds. I count to sixty and begin to rinse again. Just when I turn the shower off, I hear the door close.

Goosebumps are covering my skin from the partially

cold shower, but I ignore them while I wrap a towel around me and go into the room. Rosa has brought an entire cart of beauty products.

"I think I love you," I say and start combing through the drawers.

She laughs. "We have several of these on hand for situations like this. You're welcome to use whatever you need. There are disposable makeup pads and brushes at the bottom. Just toss them when you're done, and I'll pick this up later."

I nod and grab a few things I think I'll be able to use, then kneel down to the bottom drawer.

Rosa clears her throat. "May I ask where you're off to?"

I get back up, my hands full. "I'm not sure actually. I'm attending some corporate event with this guy I met earlier."

She takes a step back. "Oh, it's probably the Harrington mixer. All of the staff are talking about that one. Mr. Harrington flew a bunch of his employees here for a work retreat. I'm sure you're going to have a great time."

I hope she's right. Though, while I'm grateful she was quick to get me what I needed, I can't stand here and make small talk with her. I need to get ready. Not having my own things since I wasn't planning to impress anyone while on vacation is only going to make the task more difficult.

Though, my thoughts have me nearly dropping the

curling wand from my left hand. Am I trying to impress someone now? I don't want to be.

Do I?

"Are you okay, Ms. Danes?" Rosa asks, her accent heavier and showing her concern for me.

I force a smile to my face before I turn toward the bathroom. "I'm just fine. I really appreciate you bringing everything to me."

I set the newly acquired items on the counter. Then, without thinking, I drop my towel so I can put my underwear on. I hear Rosa gasp. Oops. I guess she didn't expect to see my ass when she entered my room.

My only saving grace is I got fully waxed the morning before I caught Gavin cheating. I don't have to worry about shaving my legs or anything else. Not that anything else should be a concern. I won't be showing off my goods, because I've sworn off men for a while.

So, I keep saying, and also keep contradicting.

"Fucking fuck," I mutter.

"Is there anything else I can get you, Ms. Danes?" Rosa calls. She's no longer within my line of sight. I guess she didn't want any other surprises.

"No. Thank you again," I say, assuming she'll show herself out of the room.

I don't bother to put a robe on before I towel-dry my hair, then use the blow dryer. I won't be able to get all of my hair dry, but I can tackle enough of the top layer to place some curls around my head. Anything to make it look like I wasn't just at the pool ten minutes ago.

When I turn the blow dryer off, I'm surprised to hear Rosa speaking, but I can't make out the words she's saying. I turn around to see why she's still in my room, and we nearly run into each other when she steps into the bathroom first.

"Another concierge was at your door when I went to leave. I thought it would be better for me to take the items from him for you." Rosa's holding one long box with a smaller one on top.

I assume they're both from Owen. When I peek inside the small box, I find heels, and I'm impressed he thought of them when I hadn't. I'm going to have to be extra careful with him.

I head back to the bathroom counter and reach for the curling iron. "Thank you for grabbing those, Rosa. Please leave them on the bed."

She nods and avoids my stare in the mirror, likely because I'm only dressed in a black thong and bra. The bra is boring, and the underwear are lace, but the fact that the color matches is enough.

Again, not that anyone will see them, but I'll know and that's what I'm worried about. Yep. Absolutely.

"Would you like me to wait here in case you need anything else?" Rosa asks.

I shake my head. "Thank you for everything already."

"You're very welcome, Ms. Danes." She meets my stare before disappearing from sight, and I hear the door open and close two seconds later.

I'm nearly done with my curls and check the clock. Shit, I only have three minutes left.

With no time to appreciate the dress, I rip open the box and slip the silk material over my head. The straps are wide enough to cover my bra and the cowl neckline swoops low, but not inappropriately so. The shoes are next, and somehow, they're a perfect fit, just like the dress. Something tells me Owen knows women a little too well for my liking. Though, I shouldn't be surprised after his earlier admission about why his boss hired him.

I spend the remaining minute-and-a-half I have left putting on a thin layer foundation, then adding a few swipes of mascara to my lashes. Just when I pick up the lipstick, there's another knock at my door. At least he's punctual.

I take my time coating my lips with the rosy-red color I picked and blot them before answering the door. When I do, Owen's hand is raised to knock again, but his arm freezes while his eyes rake over me.

Fuck. Me.

The heat of his stare has me clenching my thighs, and regret consumes me for agreeing to go with him. This is a terrible idea. Yet, I still don't back out.

He's wearing a charcoal suit with a crisp, white undershirt that he's left unbuttoned at the top just like earlier. I take note that he doesn't like ties, which is a disappointment. So much can be done with a tie.

I give myself a mental shake. Again.

I can't think like that. If I let myself get worked up,

I'm only going to embarrass myself. I need to figure out why men keep cheating on me before I go sleeping with any others.

Though, I can hear Kenzie's voice in the back of my head telling me that if I know he's just a fling, then what's the harm?

That's another question I don't have an answer to.

Owen's hand moves up and down without touching me, but he might as well have based on the tightening of my core.

"I'm impressed. By your earlier panic, I wasn't sure you'd be ready right on time," he finally says, then adds, "You look stunning."

I blush. "Thank you. You don't look so bad yourself."

He chuckles softly and holds out a hand. "Shall we?"

My eyes stare at his palm. If I take his offered hand, I worry I'll be branded by his touch. I know the thought is asinine, but it's one I can't stop from circling my mind.

"I don't bite, Ella."

Well, that's disappointing, I think.

Owen's voice deepens. "Though, I'm not opposed to doing so if that's what you like."

Motherfreakinghell. Did I say that out loud? Kill me right fucking now.

I try to recover by laughing. "I was kidding, Owen."

He shifts in the doorway. "Right. As was I."

"Let me grab my phone and keycard," I say before darting inside to grab the items. I pull my case back and slip the card inside, then realize I have nowhere to tuck my phone. I didn't bring a cute clutch with me.

I eye my cowl neckline and frown. The dress is too low cut to hide anything there.

Owen seems to understand my predicament and says, "I think I see pockets."

I pat my hips, and sure enough, there are two small slits in the fabric. My phone barely fits, but I'm just glad to have it on me. Being able to call for help if I need it gives me a little reassurance when I walk toward Owen again. He is a stranger after all.

He's grinning and still has his hand out. Because it seems like the proper thing to do, I accept his gesture and step forward so that I have enough room to close the door behind me. Only Owen doesn't move, so I end up with my ass nestled against his dick.

I take a slow inhale before forcing a smile to my face, pretending I didn't just feel his hard length.

"Ready?" I ask.

He grunts and finally takes a step back, but he stays close enough that he can guide my hand to wrap around his forearm while he leads the way to the elevator.

When we enter, I finally have a moment to take in the rest of my dress and the shoes. The hem of the black silk falls mid-thigh. The material hugs me enough to show off my curves, but not too tight that I'm afraid to move the wrong way.

The black heels give me an added three inches of

height and are close-toed, which I appreciate since I didn't make my pedicure appointment before leaving.

"Thank you for having these delivered," I say while glancing down at myself.

He gives me another appraising look. "I'm glad they fit."

"I'd ask how you knew my sizes, but I don't think I want to know," I reply with a forced chuckle.

Owen stiffens next to me. "My first job was working in a clothing department store."

I mentally smack my forehead. I'm making this situation more awkward than a blind date, and we haven't even arrived at the mixer. This further proves that I'm the problem when it comes to men. I need to keep my thoughts to myself and just be here to smile while standing at Owen's side.

Yes, that's safest for all parties.

When the doors open, we're on the rooftop. I hadn't paid attention when Owen scanned his card and selected our destination, so I do my best to hide my surprise.

The sun is setting, casting deep orange and red colors across the sky as it darkens above. There are twinkle lights strung around the white canopies and also between them, offering the only light I can see. A DJ is set up in the back left corner, and a wooden dance floor sits empty in front of him.

"Are you hungry?" Owen asks, gesturing to the three rows of finger foods.

I lick my lips but shake my head. "Maybe later."

"Owen, come on over here," a man bellows from the middle of the room.

"That's Jack," Owen whispers in my ear and slides his arm around my waist, pulling me flush against his side.

I do my best not to stiffen, or worse, lick him. Owen smells divine. It's a woodsy scent that is more refreshing than overpowering to my senses.

The man Owen called Jack is staring at us while we make our way to him. Even with his clearly dyed brown hair, I assume him to be in his late fifties, maybe even early sixties, based on the wrinkles deepening around his eyes when he smiles big for everyone watching.

There is a younger woman standing beside him, but she almost seems like an afterthought to him when Jack steps forward to greet us.

He reaches his hand for Owen. "Good to see you with clothes on, Owen."

The group standing around us laughs in unison, and I cringe.

"Yeah, I really should learn to take those runs of mine while wearing a suit," Owen deadpans and I snort, but nobody else laughs. Tough crowd.

Jack drags his dark gaze over to me, appraising my chest and waist before my face. "And you'd be?"

"Jack, this is Ella Danes," Owen answers for me.

"Well, Ella. You could have only landed yourself a better date if I'd gotten my hands on you first," Jack says with a wink.

It takes every effort I possess to prevent a sneer from

appearing on my face. This man is even worse than my thoughts had briefly conjured while I'd been getting ready.

I take a breath, finding my calm before speaking, and lean my head on Owen's shoulder. "I don't know about that, Jack. Owen came to me shirtless and with a tantalizing offer I just couldn't refuse. That's pretty hard to beat."

Two of the men next to us make unnatural sounds at my comment, and one or more of the women gasps. However, Jack seems to be well-versed in word combat and he's not backing down.

"A real man doesn't need to spend hours in the gym to *tantalize* a woman, Ella," he replies, giving my body another slow onceover.

The acid in my mouth burns when it's forced back down my throat, but I manage to plaster a smile to my face. "I guess that depends on the woman."

Jack cocks his head. "I guess so."

Owen shifts uncomfortably. "We're going to grab drinks. Does anyone need anything?"

Jack is still staring at me, and nobody answers Owen. I've once again made things worse, but this time I couldn't care less.

Chapter Nine

PUSH THE BOUNDARIES

Owen

I WANT TO GIVE A DAMN THAT JACK IS GOING TO have something to say about my choice in date, but I don't. Not one fucking bit. Seeing Ella unafraid of the man most people cower to has my interest in her rising by the second. I know this isn't supposed to be a real date, but I'll be a damn lucky man if it ends like one.

We get to the open bar just past the food tables and Ella stops. "Do you want me to leave?"

I recoil. "What? No. Why?"

She glances at where Jack still stands with his back to us. "I just annoyed the hell out of your boss. Not that I care, but I won't be offended if you want me to go."

"Is that what you want?" I ask. If she was only making a scene to get out of the deal that I pretty much coerced her into, then I'm not going to force her to be at my side.

I'm not a selfish prick. I want this arrangement to be mutually beneficial.

She bites the inside of her cheek, and it takes every restraint I have to keep from stroking her smooth skin.

"I don't know," she answers honestly. Something that takes me by surprise.

"Well, you let me know when you do. Just because you put on the dress and opened the door, doesn't mean I'm going to hold you to anything, Ella."

Though, I'd like to press her against the brick wall behind us and kiss her until she can't remember anything other than me, but she doesn't need to know that. Not yet, anyway.

Her cheeks flush, and I wonder what she's thinking, but I don't want to scare her off when she already seems on edge, so I don't ask like I want to.

"How about that drink you mentioned?" she says.

We step forward and the barkeep greets us with a smile. He's young. Well, at least younger than me and dressed in an all-black tuxedo. He tosses his longer blond hair back and asks, "What can I get you?"

"A whiskey sour," I answer, then nod toward Ella. I don't intend to order for her.

"Bartender's choice. Just make sure there's vodka in it."

Her answer isn't all that surprising considering she ordered something similar when we were on the plane together. Though, I also wouldn't be surprised if she normally prefers wine when she isn't nervous.

She sighs. "I think I'm going to need something stronger than wine to handle this party."

An unexpected sense of satisfaction fills me that I wasn't wrong about her normal preferences. "You're probably right."

I want to ask if by ordering the drink that it also means she's staying, but I keep the question to myself. I don't need to remind her that leaving is an option.

The bartender hands us our drinks. "A vodka tonic for the beautiful lady."

I notice her slight smile at the compliment when we step to the side, and I take note that she seems to appreciate that someone took notice of her efforts to look nice for the mixer.

Ella leans against one of the canopy frames, and her shoulders give off a slight shudder when she glances back. "I could never work for a man like that."

I know I should say something about why I've stayed with Harrington Enterprises so that Ella understands I'm nothing like Jack, but I only shrug in response to her statement. Regret for brushing her off fills me when she looks away from me and focuses on the ocean in front of us.

There's time to salvage the moment, but I miss it when I get distracted by her beauty.

My eyes study the profile of her face. Her lips are painted with red lipstick, making them appear fuller than before. Her lashes are coated in mascara she doesn't need, and cover-up diminishes the glow she had earlier from her time under the sun. Still, her natural attraction isn't something that can be easily missed.

"Ella?" I say her name with trepidation and step closer to her.

"Owen," she counters, meeting my gaze.

"Why are you here?" I ask before taking a long pull of my whiskey sour.

She chuckles. "Because you basically made me feel like I had no choice."

I shake my head. "No, not here at this party, but here in Saint Lucia."

I don't miss her shoulders going rigid or the tightening of her jaw. "I like the beach."

Her answer is forced, and she begins to drink her vodka tonic faster.

I want to press for a better answer, but given I'd ignored her last question, I don't push. This time, I change the topic. "What do you do for a living?"

She lets out a small breath. "I work in lending for a bank."

I don't know why, but I'm surprised by her answer. "Do you like what you do?"

Ella smiles, and her eyes wrinkle at the sides. "I do. My boss allows me to do what I believe is right, not only for the client, but the bank, and encourages us to speak our minds. I've been there three years and don't have any intention of leaving."

My fingers grip my glass tighter. "That must be a nice feeling."

She nudges me with her hip. "I'm sure if you found a new employer, you might know what that's like as well."

"Maybe." I half-smile.

"How many times a year do you go on trips like this?" she asks, staying close to me.

"Like this? Just once, but there are other smaller functions that happen usually every quarter. Though, we stay in the States for those. Jack likes to surround himself with people that boost his ego."

She cocks her head to the side. "Are you one of those people?"

I shrug. "I used to be. I still do what he asks because he's my boss, but I don't kiss his ass like the others."

"That's a good thing, Owen. You shouldn't sound so ashamed of that."

Ella nudges me playfully and our eyes lock. Something unfamiliar unfurls in my chest, making me want to pull her flush against my body. I reach a hand out to do just that, but she clears her throat and backs away. The moment is gone, and I'm more disappointed about that than I should be.

I've only interacted with Ella a few times, but I'm already certain I need to know everything that I can about her. My relationships may have mostly been superficial in the past, but I've always been honest. I've never made promises to a woman I couldn't keep. I've never wanted to be the reason someone went to bed with fresh tears on their cheeks.

The more I get to know Ella, the more I hope I'm able to show her that I'm different from her ex for all of those reasons.

The music increases in tempo, and the sun has fully set. Most of the guests are now a couple of drinks into the evening celebrations, so I'm not surprised to turn around and find the dance floor is beginning to fill with employees.

"Care to dance?" I ask before finishing off my drink.

Ella reaches around and sets her nearly finished tonic on the table under the canopy. "Why not."

There's a flush in her cheeks and a slow dilation in her eyes making me wonder if the alcohol is already taking effect or if she's more affected by our closeness than she'll admit with words. Either way, I don't hesitate to grab her hand and pull her across the rooftop.

Jack is still standing at the center with a crowd growing around him. Our stares meet and I nod, pretending nothing is wrong.

My only real concern is making sure Ella has a good time.

Once we're on the dance floor, I lift her hand and spin her in front of me before wrapping my other arm around her waist, forcing her to dip backward.

She squeals, and there's a wide smile on her face when I bring her back up. Our chests are pressed together from my moves, and I don't loosen my grip.

Ella raises her brow. "Someone knows how to dance. Did you also work at a studio?"

The teasing tone in her voice makes me grin. "No, but my mother loved to. She insisted that I know my way around a dance floor, that it's the only true way to a woman's heart."

I expect Ella to retreat from my mildly serious answer, but instead her smile matches mine. "Your mother was a smart woman."

Our closeness is causing the simmer inside me to grow into a blazing inferno. Though, instead of acting too boldly on my increasing desire, I hold her tighter while leading us on the dance floor. Without missing a beat, she matches my enthusiasm and keeps close to me as our feet and hips move to the music.

When the tempo slows, I keep my left hand close enough to her delectable ass that my pinky rubs over the curve at the top. My right hand keeps hers secure in its grasp, and it's hard not to pull her flush against me again.

Her eyes are bright, and the tension in her shoulders is loosening by the second. I spin her once more, dipping her further than before so that she'll be forced to lift back up faster from my momentum.

The action does exactly what I want, and my thigh ends up between her legs. Her center is pressing against my tense muscles, and I shamelessly hold her there for seconds longer than should be appropriate just so I can watch for her reaction.

I need to know the attraction I'm feeling isn't one-sided. I'm certain it's not, but the opportunity to make sure Ella doesn't stay in denial about what she wants is too good to pass on.

Her breath hitches, and I feel the weight of her body press down on my leg. I angle her toward me, and she exposes her neck. I'm not sure if the movement is purposeful or instinctual, but I take advantage.

My lips hover over her throat, fleetingly caressing the softness of her skin when I speak. "You have no fucking idea how much I wish we were alone right now."

Ella's back arches. I can't tell if she's searching for relief at the courtesy of my thigh or so her chest can press closer to me, but either way, I'm not letting her go. Not now.

"Then, let's go find somewhere we can be," she whispers in return.

Shock doesn't even begin to describe the feeling that rushes through me, but I waste no time reacting to her suggestion.

I lead Ella off the dance floor, intent on catching the elevator I can see waiting open. Instead, Jack steps in front of us.

"I figured you would be rejoining us after you got those drinks, Owen," he says, lips pressed thinly together.

Before I can respond, Ella does. "I'm sorry, Jack. That would be my fault. I begged Owen to join me on the dance floor."

Jack keeps his stare on me, completely ignoring Ella. "I'd like you to remember that you're not on vacation,

Owen. This is a work retreat paid for by me, which means you're still on my time."

"Of course, Mr. Harrington," I say, like the biggest pussy in the world.

Why the fuck I give a shit about him being angry is beyond me. Well, that's partially a lie. My parents raised me to be respectful, and telling my boss to go fuck himself at his own party wouldn't be very respectful. Though, it would be entertaining.

"I need you to—" Jack is cut off by the appearance of one of our board members, the only group of people that work within Harrington Enterprises that Jack isn't a fuckwad to.

"Good evening, Jack," Bill says.

"Well, hello, Bill. I didn't know you'd be here," Jack says with a forced smile.

"Some of the board members thought it would be a good idea to show our presence at one of these extravagant functions that you like to host," Bill replies.

There's something off about his tone, but I don't care enough in the moment to figure out what.

"Let me introduce you to some of our valued employees," Jack says before turning his back on me.

I want to say something, especially when Bill looks back at me, but Bill makes my night even better when he doesn't follow Jack.

"It's Owen, right? I remember you from the last board meeting. All of us appreciate how you stayed late to assist with everything on such short notice," Bill says, reaching his hand toward me.

We shake and I grin. "Thank you, Bill. I'm always happy to help the team."

He smiles wide. "That's good to know."

My eyes catch sight of Jack waiting. If we were a cartoon, smoke would be pouring from his ears. It doesn't matter that I'll pay for this moment somehow, I'm enjoying the hell out of it anyway.

Bill gestures to Ella, then back to me. "I'll let you and your lovely date get back to your evening. I hope to see you around, Owen."

"I hope so, too," I reply.

The mood between Ella and I might have been interrupted, but, if there had to be a disruption, I couldn't think of a better one.

The elevator is no longer waiting, so my plans of riling her back up behind closed doors are changed to doing so right here where anyone could see. That is until I realize her whole body is shaking.

"What's so funny?" I ask, searching her face.

"Jack being put in his place. I don't know that asshole from Adam, but that was great. Bill is my new favorite person."

While I agree with her, I don't want to talk about anyone else now. I pull her against my chest. "What can I do to become your favorite person?"

Ella's eyes half close, and her lips inch closer to mine.

When the elevator dings, I'm tempted to ignore it just so I can taste her first, but then we're interrupted. Again.

"Ms. Danes?" a woman says.

"Rosa?" Ella replies.

"I'm sorry to disturb your evening, but I went to retrieve the cart I brought you and I'm so sorry to tell you that your room has flooded."

"You've got to be fucking kidding me," Ella groans, but I'm not worried.

I already have another mutually beneficial proposal ready to save the day *and* our night.

Chapter Ten

BETTER SAFE THAN ITCHY

Ella

JUST WHEN I THINK MY LUCK MIGHT BE TURNING around, Rosa drops that bombshell on me. Or maybe I should take this as a sign that I'm making a mistake with Owen. I had let my slight buzz and Owen's smooth dance moves lower my guard, which led to me practically humping Owen's leg and agreeing to...well, I don't know what, but it certainly wasn't going to include keeping our clothes on. Something I normally wouldn't do after just meeting someone.

Hell, I haven't even kissed him and I'm ready for him to have his way with me. At least I was ten seconds ago. That should have been the first clue I was being an idiot, but since I didn't take the cue, I'm taking my flooded room as a hard stop to the Owen situation.

"I'm really sorry, Ms. Danes, but that's not all," Rosa says quietly.

"Is my stuff ruined, too?" I ask, stiffening my stance and stepping away from Owen.

She shakes her head. "I retrieved your bag and items before the water could reach any personal belongings, but due to the events of the week, our hotel is fully booked. We have no other rooms we can put you in, but we're happy to help you find other accommodations and refund the cost of your stay."

My throat burns from the frustration of this whole situation. I never should have come to Saint Lucia. I should have stayed home and wallowed like I wanted. Between the shit with Gavin, seeing Blake, whatever Owen is doing to me, and now a flooded room, I've found myself at a breaking point.

"Ella can stay in my room," Owen says, and my head whips around so fast that I hear popping noises.

"Yeah, that's no—" My words are cut off when my left side begins to vibrate. "I'll be right back," I say to Rosa before I pull my phone from the pocket of my dress and walk away. My swift steps take me back toward the edge of the rooftop, and I finally answer the incoming video chat.

"What's wrong?" Piper asks.

"We should have gone with her," Kenzie adds before I answer.

Seeing their beautiful faces nearly brings tears to my eyes.

"Everything was fine and then it just went to shit again," I say.

Kenzie squints her eyes and leans closer to the screen. "Why are you wearing a dress that you didn't pack? Is that music? Are you at a party?"

"Damn, Kenzie. We didn't call to interrogate her," Piper scolds, but I can see the curiosity in her appraising eyes.

I sigh and tilt the phone for a moment so they can see. "Yes, I'm wearing a dress and yes, I'm at a party, but I was just leaving when you called."

"Why?" Piper asks.

"Well, that's a little more complicated to answer."

Kenzie smirks. "We're not going anywhere."

I move the phone until I can see Owen and Rosa on my screen. "See that man and woman standing in front of the elevator?" My friends nod. "Well, that's the guy from the plane. The same one who saved me from Blake. The woman is my personal concierge who just came to tell me that my room flooded after I left and there are no other rooms available at the hotel. Owen was just offering to let me stay in his room when you called, but given I was ready to let him to have his way with me two minutes ago all because of his dance moves, I don't think that's a good idea."

"You're right, Ella. That's not a good idea," Piper says, and Kenzie interrupts her.

"The hell it's not."

Piper raises a brow. "I wasn't done speaking. It's not

a good idea because it's a fan-fucking-tastic idea. I've spent a lot of time thinking about you this week. You are always trying to make everyone else happy, Ella. It's time for you to be selfish. If your first thought was to let that sexy man have his way with you because *you* wanted him to, then you damn well better allow that to happen."

Kenzie and I both gape at Piper. For her to be the one telling me to live a little and follow my wants... Well, it has me actually reconsidering the refusal I was in the middle of giving Owen. Mostly because if his dance moves can turn me on, I can only imagine what his bedroom skills will do to me.

Maybe it wouldn't be so terrible to be forced into his room. To consider him a one-week-stand.

"Get wild with the delicious businessman, Ella. He can be your rebound. Go bounce your big titties off his face and see what happens." Kenzie jiggles her boobs for emphasis.

My skin turns ten shades of red, and I glance around. Only the bartender is close enough to hear, but he doesn't look my way. Thank fuck. Still, I turn the volume further down.

Kenzie and Piper are making great points. I don't even know where Owen is from, but given I've never seen him around Charlotte, I doubt that has to change after this week. I could let loose and let what happens in Saint Lucia stay in Saint Lucia.

We did tell Blake we were engaged. If I run into my ex again, this would help keep the story going without making me look like an idiot as well. The more I allow myself to see the positives of this situation, the more resolved I am to listen to my friends and my libido, which has been cheering for Owen all damn day.

"Do you see those wheels turning, Pipe? She's totally going to get laid tonight," Kenzie says.

Piper shushes her, but I'm already nodding. "I'm going to stay with Owen. If it's too much, I'll figure something else out tomorrow. Tonight, it's time to say fuck all the things. The good, the bad, and the delicious."

Kenzie throws a fist in the air and Piper claps excitedly.

"Go tell him and call us tomorrow," Piper says and blows me a kiss.

I do the same back to both of them. "Thank you, ladies. Love you."

"Ride or die. We got you, boo," Kenzie adds, and I end the call.

When I turn around, Owen is waiting, but Rosa is nowhere to be seen. He takes a step toward me, but I'm ready to get off this rooftop. I shake my head at him and make my way back.

I keep my face neutral while I walk through the party. The closer I get, the deeper Owen's frown becomes.

"Just hear me out, Ella. I have a suite. One with a separate bedroom and a pull-out couch. Unless you want to spend the next hour or more calling all the other hotels, which are probably also full because this is peak season for the island, then my room is the best option."

He pauses, then adds, "For many reasons. I'll even be the one to sleep on the couch."

I grab his suitcoat with both hands and pull him closer until my lips are only an inch from his. "Nobody is sleeping on the couch, Owen."

"Fuck," he hisses and stands a little taller. His eyes darken, and he licks his perfect lips while staring down at mine.

I close the remaining gap between us and slip my tongue into his mouth. If I don't act now, I'll lose the confidence I gained while talking to Kenzie and Piper.

Owen is backing us up with one hand gripping my waist, bunching the silk material between his fingers, while his other hand is hopefully searching for the elevator button.

When we stop, he pulls back just enough to speak. "Are you sure about this?"

"I've had a terrible week. I need whatever this is. Even if it's just for tonight," I answer honestly.

"I feel really bad for being thankful about your shitty week, but I can't help it," he murmurs against my mouth.

"Just make me forget everything else as soon as we're back in your room and I won't give a damn what you're thankful for," I reply and nip at his bottom lip.

He presses closer to me, and I can feel his dick against my stomach. "You'll be lucky if we make it back to the room."

"I'll be lucky if we don't," I retort with a saucy grin.

The elevator opens, and we're inside before I can take my next breath. Owen fishes the room card out of his pocket, and my fingers deftly work at the buttons of his dress shirt.

I get three buttons down before thinking a little more clearly. There could be cameras in this thing, given how fancy the hotel is. Only Owen hasn't reached the same conclusion.

As soon as he selects the option for his floor, my back is pressed against the steel wall and his hands are moving tormentingly slow up my sides until they cup each of my breasts. His thumbs rub over my nipples, and mewling noises leave my mouth.

I arch closer to him, needing his touch and no longer caring who might see.

"I knew you were special the second I saw you," he whispers against my neck before his tongue swirls over my sensitive skin.

Words want to leave my mouth, but all that comes out is a soft moan.

He pinches one of my nipples and lowers his head, but the doors open to his floor before things can escalate. I want to cry that we're going to have to move from our position, but I know the momentary pause on whatever this is will be worth it once we're alone in his suite.

Owen surprises me when he settles his arms behind my back and picks me up with ease. He carries me down the hallway while I nip at his neck.

"I don't know who called you before, but I owe them

flowers or something," Owen says when he stops at what I assume to be his door.

"My best friends Kenzie and Piper, but do you really want to talk about them right now?" I ask.

He gets the door open. "Fuck no, I don't."

We step inside the room, and I don't even get the chance to look around before my back is against the now-closed door. My legs wrap around Owen's waist, and I lock my ankles behind him. His hands slide up my dress, and he grips my ass. One of his fingers moves down my backside, lifting my panties and making its way south.

"So fucking wet already," he groans, then rubs a thumb lightly over my clit.

I buck against him. I'm not in the mood for foreplay. I need to take the edge off whatever has been simmering between us throughout the day. We can take our time later, but right now, I need his dick inside me more than I need my next breath if I'm expected to not overthink this whole situation.

I just keep trying to remind myself that this is no different than going home with someone after the first date. I've done it before, and I certainly don't slut shame others who do so more often. I deserve a night of being devoured after all the hell I've been through, and since Owen seems so willing to oblige...

I yank on the belt I spot between my quivering thighs, and he gets the point. His tongue drives into my mouth with the same eagerness I'm unable to control. His hand leaves my slick center, and he has his pants down in a matter of seconds, all while he's still tongue-fucking my mouth like a damn king.

"Condom," he mutters.

"Fuck." I have an IUD, but given Gavin was cheating on me, I can't be certain of anything. Plus, I don't know Owen. We're better safe than itchy later.

"Inner left pocket," he adds.

Oh, thank fuck he's a confident man. I reach inside his suitcoat and pull out the foil wrapper, tearing it open with my teeth.

Owen takes the condom from me and lifts me higher before sliding the rubber on. I slip down the door I'm still pressed against, and the head of his thick cock presses against my needy pussy. I push down, wet enough for him that the layer between us isn't going to be a problem.

He rises and thrusts inside me so hard and fast that I nearly come at first contact. My nails dig into his shoulders, and I groan loudly while powerful shivers travel down my spine.

I tighten my legs around his waist, and his hands grip my ribs. He's pounding into me with abandon, and I tilt my head back against the door. The action pushes my chest forward and Owen doesn't miss the opportunity to nip at my tits.

He bites through the thin fabric, and I cry out. The walls of my pussy clench around his dick, and I know I'm close already. Owen's speed increases, and one of his hands comes up enough to pull the neck of my dress down.

My nipple pops out of the bra, and he tugs the tip of my pebbled breast inside his mouth. He bites and sucks, then twirls his tongue over the sensitive area. I bite my lip and try to hold back my screams, but then he adjusts his hold on me, sending his dick even deeper inside me. No matter how much longer I want this to last, I can't keep my orgasm at bay any longer.

He captures my cries with his mouth and thrusts inside me with increasing vigor. My skin is on fire, and I'm loving every fucking second of this sexual torture. My toes curl inside the heels I'm still wearing, and my core constricts with every stroke of Owen's tongue.

All tension has left my body. My mind is free from all my earlier thoughts and worries. My neck and chest are warm, sending a tingling surge through the rest of my body.

I know right then that I have never been properly fucked, because having my vision blur, my pussy clench so painfully, and every muscle of my body ache has never felt so damn good.

Feelings I'm trying to ignore swirl between the waves of euphoria Owen has elicited from me. I don't want to care for the man who is fucking me senseless, but damn, the way he's touching my sensitive skin like he knows me better than I know myself and how his eyes haven't left mine since I began to come... It's a lot to process. So much so that I ignore the more serious thoughts trying to grow in my mind and only focus on the fact that Owen is still hard inside me when my orgasm ceases.

When my eyes can focus again, I see a smirk growing on his face. "That was fucking sexy."

He's not even out of breath, but I can't stop my chest from heaving in and out. "I need to get to the gym if I'm staying in this room with you."

"Oh, El. I'll give you all the exercise you'll ever need."

Chapter Eleven

DON'T HIDE YOUR PLEASURE

Owen

FUCKING ELLA AGAINST THE DOOR IS THE hottest thing I've ever done, and I've done some crazy shit in my days. Hearing her agree to stay with me was one thing, but seeing her come undone under my touch? That was more than I could have imagined.

Still, I'm not even close to done with Ella. Before the sun rises, I'm going to have fucked her on every surface of this hotel room. I'm going to make sure my dick is branded on her pussy—that she won't ever be able to forget me once she leaves this island.

I carry her from the door, and her head lolls against my neck, stray hairs tickling my face. I grab a fistful of them and bring her head back so I can see her face while we walk toward the couch.

Her lips are swollen from my demanding kisses, and I want them on my dick soon. Her green eyes are brighter than I've seen since we met, and there's a delicious flush covering her cheeks and chest.

"I'm not even fucking close to done with you yet," I rumble my previous thoughts roughly against her ear.

She trembles within my hands, and I finish carrying her the fifteen feet inside the room to the couch. My pants are sliding down my ass, but they stay up long enough that I can lay Ella on the sofa.

The silk material of her dress bunches around her hips, and I'm tempted to rip the fabric apart, but I hold back. I don't want to ruin the dress. I want her to keep it so that anytime she sees the silk hanging in her closet, her legs shake and pussy clenches in longing at the memories that fucking dress evokes.

She makes these sexy noises, and her hips lift once she's settled on the cushions, searching for release. I want to deny her. I want to make her beg for what I know only I can give her, but the succulent scent of her sweet center is like a siren whose call I can't ignore.

I adjust my pants so they're no longer falling down, then pull the condom from my cock that is still dripping from Ella's explosive orgasm and more than halfway off already from the walk across the room. I have plenty more protection in the bedroom for when we need it.

Ella's head tilts up. Her eyes are still bright, but there's a sheen of concern covering them now. I've waited too long. She's been able to think too much. I need to rectify the situation before she changes her mind and decides to leave.

My fingers gather the soft material of her dress and tighten until the fabric is bunched around her ribs. Using my other hand, I slide her underwear to the side just enough that I can see her glistening lips before pulling the thin black material down and out of my way.

"Fuck. You're so beautiful, Ella."

She turns away from me as if she doesn't believe my words.

I release my hold on her dress and move over the top of her, wishing I'd just pulled the condom back up rather than having removed the rubber. Instead of fucking some sense into her, I stare at her face until her delicate eyes meet mine.

"You are beautiful, Ella."

There's a shimmer of something in her eye. As much as I want to find out what happened in the past to make her believe she is anything other than perfect, I know that now is not the time.

Right now, Ella needs someone to worship her and make her forget all the bad things that have been happening. I'm more than thankful that I get to be the lucky bastard who fills that role.

I press my lips to hers, and she opens to me without hesitation. While my tongue fights for domination over her mouth, my right hand ventures south again. My fingers trail over the dips and curves of her body. First over the perfect mounds on her chest, pinching her still-hard nipples, then down her stomach, circling her belly button.

She flinches beneath me and bites my lips. This beautiful creature is needier than I realized.

My palm cups Ella's pussy, and her back arches. I slip one finger inside her, then another. My mouth captures her moan, and the taste of the vodka she'd been drinking coats my tongue.

Her hips lift in time with the pace my fingers have set, but I don't plan on finger-fucking her into her next orgasm. No, I want her to come all over my face while screaming my name.

I keep my hand pressed against her pussy and kiss my way down her neck. "Take this dress off," I demand.

Ella's hands are frenzied when she complies. Within seconds, she is in nothing more than her bra and the heels I purposely left on her.

I reach my free hand under her back and unclasp the bra. Her tits fall free from the contraption, and it's tossed to the side by my teeth.

She's clenching around my fingers still buried deep inside her. I know if I want her to come the way I envision, then I need to hurry up, but I can't help taking my time.

My tongue swirls over her left nipple, and my teeth scrape at the beaded skin before I lap at it once more. I pay the same attention to her right tit, then drag my tongue over her stomach. The tip circles her belly button and moves to the side where I suck on the sensitive skin just beneath her hipbone.

"Mother fuck," she mutters, then arcs up higher.

I pull her nearest leg up and nip at her inner thigh while I slowly withdraw my fingers from her soaking center. She whines in protest, but the sound only lasts a second, because as soon as my hand is out of the way, my mouth is covering her pussy.

The sweet taste is even better than it smells, and I have to remind myself not to come in my pants when my balls tighten. This moment isn't about me. It's about Ella and branding her with the memory of me and my dick.

My tongue flicks over her clit, then I suck on the sensitive nub until she cries in pleasurable pain. I lift her other leg into the air, placing both of them over my shoulders until her ass lifts off the couch.

Ella's hands dig into my hair, and her thighs squeeze tightly around my ears while I continue to lap at the delicacy that she is. I move my tongue from the top of her slit down as far as I can without bending her to an awkward angle.

She gasps from the unexpected move, and I slip one of my fingers between her ass cheeks, putting the slightest bit of pressure there before moving back to her perfect pussy.

"Holy hell." Her words are muffled, and I realize she's put a throw pillow over her face.

With my free hand, I rip the pillow from her grasp.

"Don't hide your pleasure from me, Ella. I want to hear my name leave your mouth loud and clear."

Her throat bobs and head nods while she licks her lips.

"Good girl."

Two of my fingers are pressed firmly over her ass when I begin sucking on her clit again. Pressing, licking, sucking, moaning, none of which I'm going to be able to get enough of. Especially not when Ella grips my hair and flails beneath me like nobody has ever eaten her pussy before.

She stiffens and lets out a warning moan. "Owen."

The sound isn't enough for me. I want to make her scream so loud that the rest of the damn resort is jealous of her pleasure.

I bring my other hand down and press my thumb over her clit while my tongue laps relentlessly at her pink flesh.

Her legs squeeze harder around my face, and her back lifts farther off the couch.

"Owen...fuck me!" she screams, bringing a triumphant smile to my lips.

I know she doesn't mean the words literally right now, but that is exactly what I plan to do next. For the moment, I revel in her sweet scent that coats my face and the way her body is still pressing closer to me even though I know it's spent.

More importantly, I know that, no matter what Ella

Danes decides she wants tomorrow, this night—this moment—will be one she can never remove from her memory.

Chapter Twelve

FUCKING MINT TOOTHPASTE

Ella

THE DOOR, THE COUCH, THE HALLWAY FLOOR, the bedroom. Shit, I think there was even an orgasm to be had in the damn kitchen. Regardless, Owen made me come so many times that I lost count, and he rebounded faster than any man I've ever known.

When I fell asleep just after three in the morning, I thought I was near death, but as the morning sun peeks through the curtains, I can't help looking at Owen's sleeping form and wanting more of him.

I know this is bad. I know that I swore off men for the time being. I'm also aware that I know very little about the man who has touched or licked every part of my body, but somehow, I feel closer to him than I have any other before him.

There's a connection between us. I felt it the

moment he sat down next to me on the plane, and it was the main reason I'd done my best to ignore him then. I would have succeeded if he hadn't been staying at the same hotel as me. Though, would I have wanted to face Blake alone? Having Owen step in and lie about our not-relationship was a shock, but now that I've had some time to think about his heroics, I'm thankful for his quick thinking.

Still, I don't want to get real feelings for this man. I need to keep things strictly sexual in hopes that being with Owen physically will help me get over my breakup with Gavin. It's a tactic I've never tried, and I'm optimistic of the outcome, as long as I can keep my emotions in check.

An idea comes over me, and I sneak out of bed to the bathroom. Wanting to stay as quiet as possible, I pull the door shut behind me before heading to the sink.

I smirk and say a silent thanks to this fancy fucking hotel when I see two toothbrushes at the sink. I grab the one still in plastic and quickly open it.

Within a minute, my morning breath has vanished, and my hair has been tamed. I don't care how many positions Owen had me in the night before, I don't want him to have any regrets when he wakes up to what I have planned.

He's still sound asleep when I creep back into the room. I gently lift the covers, and my grin grows wider when I see Mr. Unstoppable is already hard for me.

I settle myself between his legs, letting the comforter

keep me hidden. He flinches and shifts his legs, and his fingers find my hair when I reach for his rigid cock.

I'm honestly shocked he's capable of a boner this morning. I had a fleeting thought that he might need a day or two to recover, but I'm not complaining.

When Owen lifts his hips and groans, my tongue darts out, circling his thick head. One of my arms holds me up, and I use my hand from the other to cup his balls.

Owen half-chokes and moans at the contact, so I squeeze harder until his fingers tighten around my long strands. I run my tongue down one side of his veiny shaft then up the other before covering his delightful dick with my mouth, taking him as deep as my throat will allow.

His hum of approval has my head bobbing up and down faster and my fingers massaging his balls just a little tighter.

That is until he tenses beneath me. I loosen my hold and focus my efforts on his cock, but I can feel him backing up.

"Burns. Something fucking burns," he growls.

The comforter is thrown off the bed, revealing me between Owen's legs. I look up at him, confused and worried I've done something wrong.

He's looking at his junk like it's going to fall off, and I'm not sure what to do.

"Why is my dick on fire?" he practically yells, and I hope he doesn't expect me to answer because I have no fucking clue. I only got out of bed to brush my... Oh, no.

The toothpaste. The mint fucking toothpaste.

I cover my mouth, because I'm not sure if I'm going to laugh hysterically or cry in embarrassment.

"What is it? Do you see something?" Owen asks, his voice rising in panic while he lifts his cock, searching the affected area.

I try to speak, but I can't make the words leave my mouth. Instead, I roll onto my side, laughing uncontrollably while he hops around, trying to find the cause of the burning sensation.

Owen is staring at me like I've lost my damn mind, so I try to explain.

"Mint...teeth...clean."

His brows furrow deeper. "What the hell are you saying, Ella?"

I'm holding my sides, they ache so bad, and I attempt to take a deep breath. "The toothpaste."

"Why are you talking about brushing your damn teeth? My dick is in pain." Owen seems near tears, and his hands wave over his burning cock.

"I might have brushed my teeth right before I came back to bed," I finally manage to get out.

His eyes widen and jaw tightens when he finally understands, and he's running toward the bathroom before I can see if he's truly mad. I hear the shower turn on and follow him.

When I enter, he's glaring at the garbage can and holding his dick with both hands. "Fucking mint toothpaste."

I pat his shoulder. "We'll have to burn them all in

protest."

"Don't you fucking placate me. I'm going to spank your ass for that."

My face must give away the tightening of my insides, because Owen leans in until his mouth is just over my ear. "Or maybe I'll withhold your spankings."

He picks me up and carries me into the shower, then sits me in the corner against the smooth white tile. "You only get to watch."

Owen reaches for the body wash, and my shoulders are still shaking from laughter. "I really am sorry. I didn't think the toothpaste would burn."

Lesson learned. It was more important to rinse fully than be quiet.

His lips slowly lift. "Then, I think you should get over here and kiss things all better."

With a smirk of my own, I step away from the corner and under the spray of the shower. "I thought I was only allowed to watch."

"I changed my mind." Owen's hands grip my neck, then his fingers work their way into my hair.

His mouth crashes against mine, and I don't hesitate to open for him. I know this morning after is too much too soon. I also know staying with him isn't what I should be doing, but damn it, I don't want to stop whatever is happening.

Instead of putting an end to this chaos, I reach down and cup his balls, fully intending to "kiss things all better" just as soon as Owen is done tongue-fucking my mouth and making my toes curl.

———

LATER THAT DAY, I FIND MYSELF AT THE BEACH, enjoying the heat from the sunshine pouring out of the clear blue sky. I spent the morning—after properly rinsing my mouth, then blowing Owen in the shower—getting my things from Rosa before going for a massage.

With my libido sated and the rest of my body relaxed, my aim is for the water and UV rays to calm my mind. Surprisingly, I'm not as frantic as I thought I might be about Owen.

We haven't talked about what we're doing now that he's not only my fake fiancé, but my hotel roommate. A part of me doesn't want to have that conversation, because it's easier to pretend none of this is happening in real life and that last night was a one off.

If I accept that I'm going to screw Owen for the rest of the week, then I might lose whatever cool I've been able to keep.

Maybe it's knowing I have no clue where he's from and that this is short-lived that's helped me not regret last night or this morning. Or maybe it's me being dumb and allowing another man into my life only days after having my heart stomped on by douchebag Gavin.

Either way, I'm going to choose not to think too hard about things for the time being. My two closest friends seem very pleased with that. They've been texting me non-stop while they're at work, but I'm not putting anything in writing for them to screenshot and remind me of later. Especially Kenzie. I love her, but she can be pure evil some days.

"Can I get you another Sex on the Beach, miss?" my cabana boy asks.

I grin. He's been calling me "miss" since I first sat down. "I think I'm good, Sam."

His light-brown eyes and cocoa skin shimmer under the sunlight behind him. "Please, let me know if you change your mind. I'll let you get back to relaxing."

The Vistas must have the best headhunters in the business, because I've never been somewhere that had employees so eager to please, but I'm not complaining. Thanks to their helpfulness, this trip has been much easier to handle.

My phone rings, and it's a video call from Kenzie and Piper. I answer and grin at their welcome faces, assuming they're both on lunch.

"You lucky bitch," Kenzie says before I even have the chance to say hello.

"Oh, yeah. She listened to us alright," Piper adds.

"How the hell do either of you know anything?" I ask.

They're both smiling like they're the ones who got laid.

"Dude. You have the 'I've just been fucked within an inch of my life' grin on your face, and I'm jealous as hell,"

Kenzie answers, popping a chip from her lunch into her mouth.

Piper nods, her smile softening. "It looks good on you. I'm really happy for you, El."

While I appreciate their excitement for me, I don't want to make a big deal out of what's happening. "There's no reason to be happy or jealous of me. This is a vacation fling. I don't even know where he lives. He could be from Alaska for all I know."

"You didn't ask him any questions before you had sex with him?" Piper asks, clearly not impressed with my actions, or lack thereof.

"I mean, I know where he works and his last name. If I needed to track him down later for any reason, I wouldn't have a problem," I reply, now hoping like hell there won't be "any reason" for that scenario to come true.

"Where does he work?" Kenzie asks, resting the phone on something. I see her laptop come into view.

"Not telling you. You're not allowed to cyber-stalk him," I say with a laugh.

She glares at me, but there's not a damn thing she can do to me through the phone. I won't fall victim to any of her tactics.

"If you don't tell me what I want to know, then I'm going to your house to put some more of your stuff in the front yard with a free sign. Your couch is already gone, so I'm sure the other items will go fast, too."

"You wouldn't." Even as I say the words, I know she

absolutely would. Nothing expensive that would make her a bad friend, but random things I wouldn't even realize were missing until I needed them months down the road. *That* is the kind of deviousness I know Kenzie is capable of. Though, I'm glad to hear the tainted couch is forever out of my life.

"I would and you know it. Tell me where he works and his last name or I'm getting in my car," Kenzie threatens.

I look at Piper, but she only shrugs. "You know I can't stop her. Neither of us can. Just tell her."

I sigh and glare. "Harrington Enterprises and Porter."

Kenzie's eyes widen and she moves her laptop to the side. "Ella, don't freak out, but Harrington Enterprises is based right out of Charlotte."

I'm shaking my head and blinking rapidly, and no words will leave my mouth. No, that can't be right. How would I not know that? Owen made the company sound huge. If they were local, wouldn't they have appeared in the paper or on the news or *something*?

"My dad had a case that involved the current CEO. Complete dirtbag that screwed over some of his long-time employees, promising lucrative retirement accounts that never came to be when they retired."

"I had the displeasure of meeting him, so I'm not surprised to hear that, but why don't I recognize the company name?" I ask, forcing myself to take a few deep breaths. This isn't terrible, right? I've never seen Owen around. I'm sure I would have remembered if I had. There are literally millions of people in the Charlotte area. I could still never see him again after leaving Saint Lucia.

Piper flips her screen, pointing the camera at her work computer, and shows me the downtown business center owned by West-to-East, Inc. A big business that moved to town about ten years ago. I don't know what they do, but I have a sinking feeling I'm about to find out.

Piper points to her screen at the metal sign above the high-rise building. "That is the name of the main office you know. One which falls under the umbrella of Harrington Enterprises."

Son of a bitch. I'm trying to hang on to my previous notion that nothing has to change just because Owen is from my area, but my hands are shaking, my pulse is rising, and my mind is spiraling to worst-case scenarios I have no business thinking about.

I fucked up by fucking Owen Porter.

"She's losing it. We shouldn't have said anything," Piper says to Kenzie.

"No, she's going to be okay. Owen is a good guy. I already found his social media profiles. He donates to a bunch of shelters. He doesn't post nasty shit about women. He even lives in a nice house with his own car from what I can tell from these pictures. He's nothing like...those who shall not be named."

Piper cringes. "Or maybe that's the perfect front for a serial killer."

Kenzie waves one of her hands. "You've been watching TV too much. Seriously, I'm not getting any bad vibes from this guy. Has he said or done anything to make you question anything, El?"

I bite my lip and think back to our interactions. Owen was respectful on the plane. He gave me plenty of outs last night. He didn't initiate the sex, I did. Maybe he isn't so bad, but still, I can't stop from wondering if it was a terrible idea to sleep with him.

"I need to go. I love you both, and I appreciate you checking on me and sharing the information, but I came here to do things on my own and get over Gavin. I need to figure this out by myself."

Before they can try and change my mind, I end the video chat and grab my things. I need to walk, to move and think clearly. If I sit here any longer, I'll end up back on my phone and booking the first flight home. While that option seems safest, in my heart, I don't think it's the right one.

I'm barely a quarter of the way to the trail I intend to take when my phone dings several times. With a sigh, I grab it and find messages from both Piper and Kenzie.

Kenzie: *I know you weren't looking for someone else, but maybe that's exactly why this happened.*

Piper: *Kenz could be right. This Owen thing could be nothing, but from the look on your face, it could be everything you didn't know you needed.*

Don't shut the idea down before you know what it could be.

Kenzie: If you run now, you'll always wonder what if. That's a shitty way to live and you know it. Don't let those shitbag exes of yours control your decisions any longer. Do what you truly want to do.

My chest tightens, and I send a quick reply of thanks before turning off my phone and continuing toward the trail. It's time to think for myself and without distraction.

Chapter Thirteen

ALL THE DICK LOVE

Owen

I WAIT UNTIL I LEAVE THE HOTEL ROOM TO check my phone. I assume Jack is going to have something to say about my early departure the night before, but I'm out of fucks to give. I don't know what it is about Ella, but she makes me question the stupidity of having stayed employed by Harrington Enterprises even more than I have been lately.

The only thing I can't let go of now is my conversation with Bill the night before. He's here in Saint Lucia for a reason. The board wouldn't have sent a member here if everything was fine. I shouldn't want to find out what's going on, but after investing in this company for five years, I can't deny my interest.

As I scroll through my notifications, I find that Jack has called and texted me once each and only emailed twice. Surprisingly, he doesn't seem as angry as I assumed he would be. Maybe today won't be as bad as I thought.

I don't bother to call or text Jack back since I'm headed to where he should be right now, which is our first team-building activity: mini golf.

Jack is standing at the entrance to the tropical course with Mason from marketing, Todd from projects, and Natalie. Mason and Todd aren't much better than Jack, and I hope that Natalie doesn't get herself too tightly wrapped up in the company politics now that she's gotten the promotion. Then again, Jack doesn't seem too pleased with her, so maybe there's nothing to concern myself with.

"Look who finally decided to show up," Jack says with a roll of his eyes. Apparently, he doesn't have to remain professional in front of this group.

I glance at my watch. "Unless you made last-minute schedule changes that weren't emailed, then I believe I'm two minutes early, Jack."

"If you're not a half-hour early, then you're late," Jack replies and turns to Mason to mutter something.

I don't bother to try to listen. "I'll go grab my things so we can go."

Natalie steps forward, pushing her short nearly-black hair behind her ears. "I'll show you where to get the putter."

I almost tell her I don't need help, but when I look at her pale blue eyes and see the tension in her shoulders and slight tremble in her hands, I don't object.

When we're far enough away that the others shouldn't hear us, her elbow brushes against mine. "Did Bill talk to you yet?"

I keep my eyes ahead. "Nothing more than a short greeting last night. Why?"

Her hands twist together in front of her. "I found something I wasn't supposed to during an account audit. My supervisor was out of the office, so I brought the discrepancy to Jack. I wanted to tell you sooner, but Jack manipulated me before I even knew what was happening."

Fuck. This was even worse than I had thought after Jack asked me to bring Natalie to the party last night.

She glances behind us before continuing. "Bill reached out to me after my unexpected promotion was announced. He's trying to help unravel the web I've fallen into, but even I don't really understand everything that's going on. I told Bill I trust you and that you might be able to help us since you're close to Jack but not under his thumb like the other assholes who work for this company."

We round the corner of the building, and I can't see Jack any longer. My steps slow before we reach the window to get the items I'll need for the game. "What did you find?"

She lifts her head slightly and peeks around again. "I'm not even sure. All I know is there was nearly three million dollars missing from the main corporate account when I was done with my audit."

Holy shit. That isn't small. No wonder Bill made an appearance. Hell, I'm surprised more of the board didn't come with him.

"Last night, Todd wouldn't leave me alone. He was trying to get me drunk and to go back to his room. I don't know what Jack's up to, but I'm scared," Natalie adds, making my anger for the men waiting on us rise tenfold.

I can assume what Todd was trying to do, given how Jack asked me to help him take care of a problem when it came to Natalie. She deserves better than that, and I know I can't ignore this, no matter how much I wanted to at first.

"What can I do to help?" I ask.

We get to the line for the putter, and she quiets. "Let's meet up later."

I nod. This isn't something to be discussed in public, not when we're talking about the embezzlement of millions of dollars by the company CEO. While Jack might run the company, he doesn't own it. Not after he had to go public and hire a board of directors to prevent the retirement account lawsuit from going too public.

Shit, this is bad. I didn't think anything could ruin the high I was riding from last night's events and even this morning, but Natalie's admission fills me with dread. I don't want to be wrapped in the middle of something I had nothing to do with, but at the same time, this could be just what the company needs to get Jack out of the picture. This company could do so much good in the world without him running it.

Natalie steps to the side when we get to the front of the line. "A stick with one or two balls?" the young kid at the counter asks me with a smirk.

"Just one is fine." I want to find his questions funny, but despite Natalie's revelation, my mind wanders back to Ella while we wait for him to return with the items.

Aside from thinking my dick was going to fall off this morning, everything about being with Ella is more than I could have imagined.

I knew there was something exceptional about her when I saw her on the plane, but damn. The sparks between us, the attraction, natural chemistry... All of it combined is nothing like I've felt before.

I've never been the kind of guy who set out to find the one, but after last night, I already know I'm not giving Ella up easily. There is a light inside her that I want to ignite in more ways than one.

The guy returns and hands me the putter and ball. I turn with Natalie to go back to our group. We've taken too long to walk the short distance, and the three waiting jackasses stare daggers at us since we'll now be last in the lineup, but I don't pick up my speed and neither does Natalie.

"Jack wanted me to take you to the mixer last night. I'm sorry you got stuck with Todd, but I'll try to help run interference now that I know more. Though, it will only be for show and while we're at the functions," I say, still keeping Ella in mind when I say the last bit. I don't want this situation to leak outside of work, not when I've just met Ella and want to spend as much time with her as possible before our week is up on the island.

She smiles and nods. "Thank you, Owen."

I'm not sure I've made the right choice by basically telling Natalie that we need to pretend to be into each other while we're around Jack, but as long as she understands, I go with the plan for now.

We return to the group, and Jack is eyeing the two of us. I can only hope that's a good thing, but knowing Jack, he could have already changed his mind from the night before.

Jack grabs my arm when I attempt to walk past him. "Everyone go ahead. Owen and I will be right behind you."

I don't let my aggravation show and keep my face neutral. "What's going on, Jack?"

He moves so his back is to the others. "We need to chat."

"Is this about the messages you sent? My phone died and I didn't realize the charger wasn't plugged in all the way," I lie and take a step away from his closeness.

Jack dismisses my words with a wave of his hand. "Don't worry about last night. I'd rather not see that date of yours around anymore, but I'm more concerned with Natalie. I mentioned that I was having a problem with her, and her showing interest in you just now tells me I was right to ask for your help. Be nice to her. See if she'll tell you anything for me."

"What topic should I be hoping she'll mention something about?" I ask with a tilt of my head.

Jack drums his fingers over his thigh. "That's not important. Just let me know if she says anything out of the ordinary, okay?"

"Sure, Jack. I'll see what I can learn and get back to you," I say with a grin.

————

EIGHT PAINFUL HOURS LATER, I'M ABLE TO HEAD back to my hotel room. Mini golf lasted three of those hours, then there was lunch where it seemed like everyone except for Natalie and I got drunk before we headed out on a yacht. Half of the employees ended up hanging out at the sides of the boat because they were so sick, including Natalie who I had to help back to her room.

She'd never been on a boat in the ocean and had no idea she'd get seasick, but I promised to find time to chat with her tomorrow when she was feeling better. With Jack wanting me to get information from her, I figured an opportunity to talk with her privately would be easier to make happen now.

Overall, the day was a shitshow, and I'm ready to see Ella in hopes she's had a better one that will rub off on me.

Except when I get to the room, she's not there. There's not even a note from her. I think back to the morning, and we definitely said dinner around seven. It's 6:45pm. Maybe I'm supposed to meet her downstairs.

I don't waste time thinking about it. I head for the shower and rinse the fucked day off me before putting on cargo shorts and a plain white t-shirt.

I'm disappointed Ella isn't waiting in the room for me when I'm done, but I don't let that deter me. I make my way downstairs and to the restaurant.

Ella isn't in the lobby, and my faith that I'm going to find her is dwindling.

A hostess greets me. "Do you have a reservation, sir?"

"No, but someone might already be here waiting for me. Her name is Ella Danes."

She looks over a sheet on the podium in front of her. "What's your name?"

"Owen Porter."

She frowns and points to the paper. "Sorry, Mr. Porter. I don't see her name or yours on our list and we put everyone here, even if they don't have a reservation."

Is Ella Danes standing me up? I didn't think she would do that, but this just proves I don't know her as much as I'd like to.

"Thank you anyway," I say before walking outside.

Maybe I've been duped. Or maybe I felt a connection with Ella that was only one-sided and she decided to take off today, regardless of the night and morning we had. I'm suddenly feeling used, and I'm not sure what to think about that. Part of me feels proud of her. I didn't think she was capable of such an act, but the other parts of me feel betrayed.

I consider going back to the room to order room service when I'm stopped in my tracks. Ella is sitting on the beach. I don't know how I see her or how I know it's her, but I just do. Her back is to me, and her brunette hair is blowing in the slight breeze brought to shore by the ocean.

Without thinking, I cross the empty road and approach Ella. She doesn't seem to hear my incoming footsteps, and when I place my hand on her shoulder, I immediately regret the action.

Ella's arm lifts, and her fist connects with my balls and dick. I land on my knees, groaning and damn near tears while sharp pains shoot from my groin through the rest of my body.

"Oh my gosh, Owen! I'm so sorry." Ella's hands are rubbing over my back while I'm hunched over in the fetal position on the sand and turned away from her. "I didn't know who you were. You scared the hell out of me," she adds when I don't immediately say anything.

"So your first thought was to cripple me?" I finally groan.

She snorts. "In my defense, you touched me without saying anything. How was I supposed to know you weren't a creeper?"

"I'm beginning to think you don't like my dick as much as I thought," I say between winces.

"I've got all the dick love for this little guy," she replies, and I can hear the smile on her face.

I cough and groan some more before I roll over to face her. "Little guy, huh? Your words aren't helping me feel better, Ella."

Her face is bright red, but her eyes are alight with amusement. "Who said I'm trying to make you feel better?"

"Touché. Now help me stand so I can make sure my legs still work. Clearly, I no longer have a need to use my dick this week if that's how you're going to treat him."

Ella wraps her arms under mine and helps me up while she's still chuckling from my pain. Her closeness is enough of a distraction to my cock that he's already reacting to merely having her hands on me.

"I thought maybe you left," I say when I'm on both feet again.

Her face darkens, and any humor we've been sharing is gone. "We should talk."

Three words no one ever wants to hear.

Chapter Fourteen

AN EVEN BIGGER FUCKBAG

Ella

I DID A LOT OF THINKING ON THE BEACH AFTER I got off the phone with Kenzie and Piper. My walk was exactly what I needed, and my mind is clearer than it has been in days.

While I still think my earlier panic was justified, I've come to the conclusion that it was also unnecessary. I'm a grown-ass woman, and just because Owen lives in the same area as me doesn't mean we're going to jump into a relationship that I'm not ready for. Plus, if I'm going to prevent the same shit from happening over and over again, then I need to learn to say what's on my mind instead of holding back.

I've never had the vagina to do that in my past. So, this is me being a new woman who doesn't get cheated on and left damaged.

"What do you want to talk about?" Owen asks hesitantly as we walk across the beach, farther from the hotel.

"Not to get all crazy on you, but about whatever this is." I gesture between us. "I have a few things to say. Things we probably should have talked about before getting naked last night."

Instead of turning and running away, Owen's lips turn up into a smile. "Not that I have any regrets about last night, but I can understand where you're coming from. Let's talk."

"I was talking to my friends about you."

Owen waggles his brows. "I hope you only had good things to say."

I shove him lightly and shake my head. "Not the point here."

He chuckles. "Of course not. Please, forgive my interruption."

I can't stop the smile that grows on my face. Owen is almost too easy to be around. The way he makes me feel so comfortable scares me, but still, I continue.

"They mentioned that your work is based in Charlotte, something I didn't expect to hear since that's where I live as well. When I agreed to stay with you, I thought this would be nothing more than a vacation fling. When I heard we lived near each other, I worried that would change things, but I don't want it to. I want to be upfront and let you know I'm not looking for anything more than whatever amazingness last night was."

I pause to see if he's still with me. His face is resolute, and he's not really looking at me as we continue toward the boulders up ahead on the beach. His lack of reaction isn't making me feel better, so instead of staying quiet like I should, I begin to ramble.

"I don't want to date you, Owen. I don't need you to pretend this is anything more than what it is. I just want you. For the next four days. When we go home, I'm sure we'll never see each other again, and that works for what I need right now. I need to know that you're okay with that and that you know I'm not going to be a stage-ten clinger."

I've said more than I intended, but it's probably best to get everything out in one go or I wouldn't have said it all. There are several ways this conversation could go, but I'm hoping Owen will think this is the greatest thing any woman has ever said to him, or he'll think I'm lying about only wanting a fling and run for the hills. Either way, I get what I want in some form or another.

Owen stops us, and my toes start to sink into the cooling sand. He settles his hands on my hips and smiles. "That was quite the declaration."

"I'm quite the woman," I say. Though I don't really believe my words, I need him to. I need him to see the person I want to be, not the pathetic woman I was just last week. I need to be better for myself. I need to work on believing in me.

"Yes, you are, which is why I'm a little disappointed about what you want. Or, more specifically, what you don't want, but I respect that you were upfront. That makes me want to be as well," he says, and I tense, looking over his shoulder at the cliffs behind him.

"I like you, Ella. It doesn't matter that I've only just met you. I was hoping we would get to know each other and see where this went even when I wasn't aware that you lived so close, but even though this isn't what I preferred, I don't care. If letting you have your way with me is the only option that I have to spend time with you, then I'm not going to complain." He pauses and smirks. "Though, my dick might stop performing if you hurt him a third time."

I laugh, glad he's broken the tension. "I'll do my best to be gentle with Owen, Jr."

Owen strokes my arm with his knuckles. "He appreciates that, but I'm serious, Ella. I won't demand something from you that you don't want, but you need to know, I also won't hide how much I'm beginning to crave you."

My chest constricts, and I'm torn between running away or jumping Owen right here on the beach. This is more than I need right now, but I can't deny that the connection between us is unlike anything I've ever experienced. That alone should scare me away from him, but I'm still resolved to keep this as a vacation fling if he's game.

Kenzie was right. I don't want to live with any what-ifs, and Piper was right, too. I'm so tired of being afraid of everything that I fail to remember how to put myself first.

"Thank you for understanding and being honest yourself," I say.

He turns me toward the setting sun and wraps his arms around my waist. "I don't like games, Ella. Remember that in case you change your mind about extending whatever this is beyond your vacation."

I try to lose myself in the purple and orange colors mixing in the sky in front of me, but I can't ignore how his words send shivers down my spine.

"What did you do today?" he asks, resting his chin on my shoulder.

"Went for a walk on the trails and spent a lot of time on the beach. Nothing exciting. How was mini golf?" I turn so I can see him and notice a bit of tension around his eyes.

"I don't want to talk about work. How about we go back to the room and order room service?"

I want to question his odd reaction, but I'm the one who said I didn't want to get serious with this. If he doesn't want to share about his day, then that's fine.

"Room service sounds perfect," I answer, and the next thing I know, I'm tossed over his shoulder and he's carrying me back toward the hotel. I squeal but relax in his arms and do my best to leave my worries on the beach.

Whatever we're doing not only feels right, but it's helping me forget the betrayal of Gavin. My biggest hope is that the strength I'm finding here continues to grow, even when I go home to an empty house.

We get to the elevator, and Owen finally sets me down. He doesn't even wait for the doors to fully close before he has me pressed against the wall and his hands grope my ass.

Our lips meet, and everything about the kiss is frenzied. Our tongues battle for dominance, our teeth clash, and our chests press together. I don't understand how he makes me feel so much with just the stroke of his tongue, but I'm not mad about it.

It takes me nipping at his lower lip for him to take a breath. "One of us should press the button for our floor," I say.

He groans before yanking the room key from his front pocket. While he handles the screen, I push my hand down his shorts. My fingers wrap around his dick, pulling and squeezing and fondling.

My thumb rubs over the tip, and I grin when it's already wet.

"I want to fuck you right here, right now, but I also don't want to get kicked out of the hotel if someone gets on the elevator," Owen says before kissing his way down my neck.

As if he conjured the event, the elevator dings and an older couple is waiting to get on. Owen moves so his back is to them and I pull my hand from his shorts.

His whole body is vibrating with silent laughter while I'm dying on the inside. I stay hidden behind

Owen, but apparently that doesn't work for the great-grandmother-looking woman who steps into our bubble, peeking around Owen's shoulder.

"Honey, don't be ashamed he couldn't wait to get back to the room. What do you think we were just doing in ours? We didn't even make it to dessert before we needed privacy. Damn oysters."

Owen chuckles. "It's always the oysters."

The doors open again to another floor, and she winks at me. "Have fun, kids. We're going dancing."

I move so I can see better around Owen. The elderly couple is already outside the elevator, and I don't miss when the husband grabs her ass on the way out. She squeals like a teenager instead of the eighty-year-old I assume her to be.

"Did that really just happen?" I ask, voice filled with disbelief.

"They're who I want to be when I grow up," Owen says, and the doors close once more.

"Why would you ever want to grow up?" I joke before reaching for him again.

Owen moves in to kiss me. All too soon, we arrive at our floor and have to pull apart again. He picks me up and cradles me in his arms.

This feels too intimate after the conversation we just had, but I ignore the heaviness in my chest and laugh when he begins to run down the hallway toward our room.

I take the key from his hand and open the door

myself, so he doesn't have to set me down. Just when I twist the handle, Owen mutters, "Shit."

"Ella?" I hear Blake's voice and really want to ignore him, but Owen turns with me still in his arms.

"Oh, look, honey. It's your friend Blaine."

"Blake. My name is Blake," he corrects with a tightness in his voice.

I look over at Cammie. Her eyes are red, but she manages to force a smile to her face. "You two are so adorable together."

Jesus, the need to warn her about Blake, regardless of whether they're already married, hits me right in my gut. If she's hoping he'll change, she's sorely mistaken.

"Awe, thanks. I'm pretty lucky." I pat Owen's chest lovingly, then without thinking too much about it, I add, "I'm getting a pedicure tomorrow at eleven. You should join me."

Blake glowers at me. "We're busy."

Well, he's sure changed his tune from when he was suggesting we have dinner together.

Cammie pats his arm. "I don't want to watch you play golf. I'll go with Ella, so you don't have to listen to me whine when I'm bored. This works out perfectly."

Blake doesn't agree, but he doesn't shoot the idea down either. Hopefully, she's able to follow through without letting him change her mind.

"Well, we were just...uhhh...going inside," Owen says.

I almost forget he's still holding me. I'm probably getting heavy, but he shows no sign of strain.

Cammie laughs. "Right. Us too. I'll see you tomorrow, Ella."

Blake drags her away and hisses something in her ear that has the smile dropping from Cammie's face.

I frown. "I feel terrible for her."

"Are you ready to tell me what happened with that guy yet?" Owen asks while he gets the door open and closes it behind us. The mood from the elevator is gone, and I wiggle out of his grasp.

"Blake cheated on me and I called off our engagement when I found out, but it was a long time ago and not a big deal now," I say, walking into the living room.

"Well, he's an even bigger fuckbag than I thought before. Only an idiot would cheat on someone as perfect as you," Owen replies and turns to his drink cart.

I snort and mutter, "I seem to only know idiots."

"What?" He turns back to me when I sit on the couch.

I hadn't meant for him to hear my words. I don't want him to know I'm damaged goods. He stalks toward me, and I'm not sure what to do other than sink further into the cushions.

Owen kneels before me and strokes my cheek. "Ella, why did you come to Saint Lucia alone?"

My throat burns and hands shake while my eyes

begin to water. I can't tell him. I can't let him see the woman who's unable to keep her man satisfied.

He grips my chin lightly. "I'm sorry, Ella. I didn't mean to pry, but you need to know that whatever happened in the past, none of that was your fault. Everything about you is perfect. In the bedroom, on the outside, and most importantly, on the inside."

I force myself to nod when I can't find the will to speak. I'm afraid if I open my mouth, the tears will finally fall and Owen will run for the hills like I'd expect any sane man to do.

He stands and leans forward to kiss my forehead. The action is quick but warms my skin all the way to my toes. Damn him for making me feel so much when I'm trying not to.

There's a tingling in my chest as I listen to Owen walk back to the drink cart. I try to focus on what's in front of me, but nothing comes into focus while my thoughts run rampant. I sit straighter and press my hands over my face, swiping my fingers when I feel my clammy skin.

Damn it, I wish we were still in the elevator. Those moments are what I need. Not ones that make me face the war happening inside me.

Okay, that's probably a lie. I decided to come to Saint Lucia so I could get over Gavin quicker. Being forced to feel this way is probably good, even if I don't like it.

Owen brings me a vodka tonic and sits next to me. "Are you okay?"

I down half of the drink in one gulp before I answer. "Peachy fucking keen."

"I haven't heard that one since high school." He chuckles, then lifts my feet up until they're settled in his lap. He unclips my sandals and tosses them on the floor.

I'm about to ask what he's doing when his thumb presses into the ball of my foot and I nearly die. "Holy fuck me," I moan, and my head falls back onto the armrest while my chest heaves. I don't know what he's doing, but I don't want him to stop.

"I don't like to see you upset, Ella. I know I can't change the past, but I can do my best to make you forget what happened for a short time," Owen says with a soft smile on his handsome face.

I moan when his knuckles rub up and down the center of my foot while I attempt to ignore his more serious declaration. "I'm turning into butter."

He smirks. "I can work with butter."

"Of course you can." I groan and arch my back over the couch.

Owen releases my foot and leans over me. "You'll find I can work with a lot of things when I want something bad enough."

A vice closes around my chest, but before I can ask what he means, Owen's tongue is sweeping against my lips and his hands are making me forget more than just my past.

Chapter Fifteen

YOU MAKE IT SO HARD

Owen

I'M BEGINNING TO THINK I NEED TO PUT MY dick on time out. This is the second morning waking up next to Ella after having spent the night ravishing her, and he's still hard as a fucking rock. I shouldn't be complaining, but I'm afraid Ella might start to.

I sneak out of bed and head to the shower. I have a couple of hours before I need to head down for brunch with my co-workers. After that, we're all supposed to go ziplining together, but until then, I'm hoping to spend my free time with Ella.

After learning we live near each other, I'm not thrilled about her declaration to keep whatever is happening between us on the island. I'd rather continue getting to know her once we're home, but maybe I can change her mind over the next few days.

It's not like we're children. We've both had life experiences that have taught us possibly more than we want to know. For me, they've taught me to go after what I want. Waiting only results in disappointment. I don't want to wait with Ella, but I'll be as patient as possible until she realizes I'm not like most other guys.

She didn't outright say the words, but her actions spoke volumes when she admitted Blake had cheated on her. The fear in her eyes when I asked why she was on the island alone said he hadn't been the only one to make Ella feel less than.

I wanted to rage on her behalf, but instead, I set out to make her forget the pain, even if it was only for the night. She accepts my distractions almost too easily, and I try not to worry about that more than necessary.

Instead, I step into the shower determined to find a way to show Ella that she's worth more than those fuckbags have deserved, but I also need to figure out how to do that in a way that doesn't scare her off.

Ideas start forming when I hear the bathroom door open and close. Ella is naked and glaring at me.

"I didn't agree to share a bed with you just so I could wake up alone," she pouts.

I push the glass door to the shower open. "Let me make it up to you."

She holds up a condom. "I was hoping you'd say that."

Maybe I don't need to worry about too much sex when it comes to Ella.

When she's close enough, I yank her into my arms. She yelps and weakly tries to fight back, but I know what she wants and I'm going to give her that and so much more.

I take the condom from her fingers and have it on within seconds. My hands slip between her legs and the warmth I feel there isn't just from the hot water.

"Always so ready," I murmur against her lips.

"You make it so easy," she replies saucily.

"And you make *it* so hard," I counter with a smirk.

She starts to laugh, but the sound is cut off when I lift her up and press her against the tile wall. I don't give her a second to prepare before I plunge inside her slick heat.

Her pussy contracts hard around my dick, and I'm sure she's going to break him, but I don't stop. My thrusts are hard and fast. Her nails are digging into my shoulders, and I know she's already close. Her perfect tits bounce in my face, and I lean forward to pull one of her taut nipples into my mouth.

She tightens painfully around me, and I know I'm not much further behind her. I increase my pace, driving deeper inside her, fueled by the moans coming from Ella's lips.

"Holy fuck," she cries when I bite at one nipple before moving onto the other.

Ella uses my shoulders to meet my thrusts, grinding harder against me. "So close."

"Right there with you," I murmur.

My hand sinks into her tangled hair, gripping the strands and pulling her face toward mine. Her lips part for me instantly, and our tongues collide. I'm ready to go at any moment, but I wait for Ella.

The hand holding her ass up moves lower until my fingers slip between her cheeks. The action catches her by surprise, and as my middle finger presses against her ass, Ella's head tilts up and she ignites around me.

After a few more hard thrusts, I'm coming right along with her. My legs lock and shivers start in my balls, then race through the rest of my body while my chest heaves in and out. I stroke Ella's hair back from her face and wait for her eyes to focus again.

"So fucking hot," I whisper before capturing her mouth.

Ella grins between kisses. "I don't know how you found so many of my detonate buttons, but I'm not mad about it."

"That's my secret to keep," I reply before smacking her ass and letting her slide off me.

I toss the condom to the corner of the shower to be picked up once I'm done, then I lather up while Ella gets her hair wet.

Her eyes are closed, the water running over her face and chest. Watching her, I know I'm fucked. Letting her go isn't an option I'm going to be able to accept easily.

She steps out from under the water and grabs the shampoo before she realizes I'm staring. "What? Do I have something on my face?"

I shake my head with a grin. "No, but if I'm lucky, you'll have my dick there later."

She glances down at my still-hard cock. "That can be arranged."

I huff, wishing that moment could be now, but I don't want everything we do to be sexual. "I have some free time this morning before I need to head out for the days' events. Did you have anything planned?"

She thinks for a moment. "Only the pedicure at eleven that I'm hoping Cammie will join me for."

I raise my hands to help Ella finish rinsing the soap from her hair. "Do you think that's a good idea?"

It's not really any of my business, but I don't want to see Ella get hurt by getting too close to the past that hurt her.

She nods. "Seeing her upset last night triggered a sense of...I don't know what, but I feel like I have to make sure she knows the truth. I'm not Blake's old friend like he told her, and I doubt he's being faithful to her even though she's beautiful."

I pull her close. "He's a selfish idiot, Ella. You can't change men like him. You are stunning and he stupidly cheated on you. There's nothing you can do to change him. You only need to know that his actions were no reflection on who you are."

Her eyes water and her lips tremble, but she sucks in a deep breath and nods. "I'm trying to remember that, but I also think that Cammie needs someone to tell her the same."

I won't argue with her. I can see her reasoning. I just hope it doesn't bite her in the ass.

"You're a better person than I am," I say before switching spots with her in the shower and rinsing myself off next.

She waves off my compliment before opening the shower door when I turn off the water. "What do you want to do this morning?" she asks.

I consider several options, but the one that stands out the most is staying in and getting to know her more. Though, I know she didn't fly all this way to be cooped up, so I give her options.

"We could stay here and play board games that I saw under the TV, or we could get out and see more of what the hotel has to offer."

Ella dries off with her towel. "I did a lot of walking yesterday. I'm good with staying in if you are."

I ease into a smile. "Sounds perfect since I'm sure I'll be doing a lot of hiking for ziplining."

"At least your business trip isn't full of meetings," she says before wrapping the towel around her hair.

I nod. "Though, I'd like to have one with Bill."

"That's the board member who showed up at the mixer?" Ella asks.

I wait to answer until my white shirt is pulled over my head. "Yeah, I heard he's looking into some shit Jack has done. Things that will give the board grounds to fire him. I didn't want to get involved, but after five years with the company, I can't help from being a little curious. Harrington Enterprises could do a lot of good if we had someone running the business who isn't only out to make a profit."

She cocks her head to the side. "Is that someone you?"

I shudder. "Hell no. I don't want to run a business that huge and feel married to my work, but I wouldn't say no to a role that allows me to make more of a difference," I answer honestly.

Ella finishes getting her shorts buttoned and then says, "My friend told me Jack got into some trouble a while back when he failed to come through on some retirement accounts."

I'm surprised she knows that considering how much money Jack paid to keep that lawsuit quiet, but I don't show it. "Yeah, that's why we have the board of directors now. Jack no longer has full control of his company. It was either that or bankruptcy. He screwed with the wrong people."

"Well, hopefully Bill being here is a good sign," she says.

"I'll quit otherwise." And for the first time, I truly mean it. I'm ready for more positive changes in my life.

Her brows raise. "Really?"

"I meant what I said before, Ella. I don't enjoy working for him, but I see potential in the company under the right leadership. I'll give it some more time, but I'm ready to be done and put my skills to use somewhere that will do more good in the world."

Something flashes over her face, but before I can figure out if the look is good or bad, I pull her into my arms. "But enough of my work. You finish getting ready for the day and I'll get the first game set up."

Her eyes brighten and she nods. "I just need five minutes."

I smack her ass when she turns back for the bathroom. "I'll be counting."

Chapter Sixteen

OKAY OWEN

Ella

AFTER OUR SEXY TIME IN THE SHOWER AND
Owen's admissions about his work, we ended up playing
three games: Connect Four, Battleship, and Go Fish.
With every win, sunken ship, and paired card, Owen
decided we should ask each other questions.

I was hesitant at first, but after the first few questions
were kept simple like our favorite colors, foods, and
things to do, I loosened up. I expected Owen to dig
deeper after a while, but instead, he took his inquiries
easy on me.

I'd thought I'd been more grateful for that, but him
being respectful of not pushing me too far was almost
worse than sharing my deepest secrets with him. His
actions showed me that he'd been paying attention to me
and really listening to me. That alone had my heart

expanding in ways I'm not sure I like, but I do my best to ignore the growing feelings I have for Owen.

By the time Owen leaves for his work brunch, I don't have much time before my pedicure.

As I grab my purse and double check everything I need is inside, chaste thoughts of Gavin enter my mind. Mostly because I haven't mourned the end of our relationship as much as I expected. I wonder briefly if that's just because I've kept myself busy with Owen or because there's a part of me that knew Gavin wasn't the one.

The conversation he freaked out over? He clearly hadn't heard the whole thing, because I remember it well. Piper had asked me if I thought Gavin might propose, and the look on my face said all she needed to know.

I absolutely wouldn't have wanted to say yes, but I might have if he did because I would have thought it was the right thing to do after two years together.

Now, being here, sort of on my own but with Owen at the same time, I'm slowly realizing that I do, in fact, deserve better than a dickass like Gavin.

A voice in my head considers if Owen could be that someone, but I ignore those thoughts. I'm open to whatever happens this week, but beyond that, I can't let those thoughts in. My near panic attack while thinking about my cheating exes the night before proves that I'm not ready to truly move on.

A knock sounds on the door, and I answer it to find Rosa on the other side. She grins widely and nods. "Hi,

Ella. I'm so glad I caught you today. I wanted to make sure the trip is still going well given the room situation."

I open the door farther to let her in, but she stays in the hallway. "Absolutely. I spent some time down at the beach yesterday, and today I'm going to the pedicure appointment you set up for me."

She pulls a pen and paper from her back pocket and scribbles something down that I can't see. "What about the windsurfing? Do you think you'll check that out soon?"

I hadn't thought that far ahead, but it sounds fun, and I've heard several people talk about it, so I figure why not. "I think I will. Thank you so much, Rosa."

Her lips thin momentarily. "I feel like I haven't done much of anything, but you're welcome. I'll check on you again tomorrow if I don't hear from you before then."

I smile and nod, watching her hurry off to likely check on the other guests she's assigned to help.

Once Rosa is gone, I circle back and grab my purse so I can head out for my appointment. It's still a little early, but I don't care. I again wonder if Cammie will show up to join me for a pedicure. I'm not entirely sure how I'll broach the subject about Blake, but the urge to do so however I can is strong after seeing her upset last night.

The spa is on the thirteenth floor, so I scan the card and press the option when it pops up on the screen. The ride down is quick, and I consider taking a detour to go check out the indoor pool since I'm a little early, but I see a curtain of blonde hair and maintain my current direction.

Cammie is sitting on a bench outside of the spa doors with her head down and hands covering her face.

I kneel and touch her knee. She gasps, then straightens her shoulders while swiping furiously at her tears. "Oh, Ella. You're early. What a nice surprise."

"And you're not okay. What's going on?" I ask.

"Nothing. Everything is fine."

Her words are spoken too quickly, and the tears still falling from her eyes prove she's lying, but I don't push. We'll have time for that soon enough. I'll try to find a way to connect with her first. I'm familiar with feeling lost, and I hate to see that same vacant look in her eyes that I've seen in my own before.

"Well, let's head inside then and see if they're ready for us," I say with a smile.

Her shoulders sag, and she follows me through the glass doors. In front of us is a reception desk with a waterfall rock wall behind it. The young man behind the desk greets us with a jovial wave.

"How may I help you lovely ladies today?" he asks.

"I have an appointment at eleven for a pedicure under Ella Danes," I say, then turn to Cammie. "Did you make an appointment after we talked?"

Her eyes widen and she shakes her head.

"Oh, that's not a problem. We have few extra openings today for spa services. Do the two of you want to be in the same room?" the receptionist asks.

"That would be great," I answer.

He asks for Cammie's room number and name, then types away on his computer. "Perfect. Follow me this way."

He guides us down a short hallway before turning right to go down another much longer section with doors on both sides of the wall. "You'll be up here on the left, door number three."

"Thank you so much," I reply when he opens the room for us.

Inside, the walls are painted a seafoam green and there are three pedicure chairs on one wall. The other is covered with shelves holding all the needed supplies.

"Get comfy. Your expert beautifiers will be right in," the receptionist says before closing the door behind him.

Cammie is still quiet when she sets her phone down and begins taking off her strappy heels.

I only have flipflops on, so I kick them off and set my purse next to me.

The soaker tubs are already filled with hot water and swirling from the jets like a mini hot tub, so I don't hesitate to stick my feet in. Cammie follows my movements and leans her head back against the seat.

Her silence makes me think this next hour is going to be either incredibly awkward or it's going to be exactly what she needs. I wanted to wait for the perfect opening to broach the sensitive subject about my history with Blake, but with how quiet she's being, I worry if I wait too long, the moment will pass. So, I do what I do best when I'm nervous. I blurt the words out.

"I was engaged to Blake five years ago." I look over at her to watch her expression, but it's the complete opposite of what I expect.

She chuckles softly and smiles at me. "Of course you were."

"I'm serious, Cammie. I don't know why Blake told you we were friends. We're not. Before first meeting you, I hadn't seen him since the day I found out he was cheating on me."

She sighs and folds her hands over her stomach. "You're not telling me anything I didn't already assume. Though, the engaged part does surprise me. Not because of you, but because of Blake."

"Why did you want to hang out with me if you knew I was his ex?" I ask.

Her sad blue eyes meet mine again. "Because I wanted to meet the woman smart enough to get away from him."

"What does that mean?" If Blake is hurting her, I'll kill him with my bare hands and feed his corpse to the sharks. I'd do that for any woman being abused.

"Blake doesn't love me, Ella. I don't know the man you were engaged to, but I don't think I married the same one. Blake only wanted me as his wife because of who my father is. He purposely got me pregnant, and I felt like I had no other choice. Now, Blake stands to take over my father's investment firm in a few years, and I get to be the lowly wife at home who takes care of the children."

Her fingers spread over her stomach. She isn't showing, but I believe the sincerity in her soft tone.

"How did all of that happen?" I ask, even though it's none of my business.

"I brought my dad lunch one afternoon and met Blake. He charmed me, sending flowers to my house that next day and begging for a date. I agreed, because what female wouldn't, right? My father even approved. We dated for a month before things started to get weird. I tried to break things off, but he blamed his off-ness on stress from work. Two weeks later, I'm pregnant, even though we'd used a condom every time. That was six weeks ago."

I gape at her. "You got married that quickly?"

"My father is a very traditional Southern man. The idea of a bastard grandchild didn't sit well with him, and because Blake had kissed his ass so severely, my objections fell on deaf ears. I either complied or I would have found myself trying to figure out how to raise a child with no support. I couldn't do that to this baby."

My hands tighten on the arm of the chair, and I force my lips closed before I say something I have no business saying, like suggesting she murder Blake for what he did.

I don't presume to understand how hard this situation is for her. I'm not a mother and I've never had controlling parents, but after a few deep breaths, I can see why she felt she had no other choice.

"I hope you intend to make his life hell," I finally say with a small smile, trying to ease some of the anxiety floating around the room.

There's a shimmer of tears in her eyes again. "You know, I didn't think of that, but I'm sure there's a few things I can do to make Blake regret targeting me."

"Girl, you have all the power here. Don't you forget that. While Blake's off doing whatever or whoever he wants, you do the same. Find a way to make your own path and get the fuck away from those toxic people as soon as you can."

A few tears fall down her cheeks. "Thank you, Ella."

"You're welcome. And, if you ever need it, don't hesitate to reach out to me for help. I'm sure we don't live too far from each other unless Blake moved away from Charlotte. That bastard doesn't deserve to get everything he wants."

She laughs through the tears. "No, he certainly doesn't. At least you seem to have done better with your second choice in fiancé. Owen seems perfect for you."

I don't want to lie to Cammie anymore, so I merely nod in reply. If she lets me help her, then I'll come clean about Owen, but in the meantime, that's my little secret. I do hope she'll reach out or at least take my advice. Her kid deserves that just as much as she does.

———

A FEW HOURS LATER, I FEEL LIKE A QUEEN walking out of the spa. Cammie only stayed for the pedicure, which disappointed me. We were having fun once we stopped talking about the heavy stuff. I, however, opted for the offered manicure and sixty-minute massage afterward.

It's been too long since I've been pampered, and I decide that I'm going to demand monthly spa days with Kenzie and Piper when I get home. We shouldn't only treat ourselves when we go somewhere special.

I head to the lobby in search of some coffee and maybe a little sunshine. When I get to the coffee bar, I hear familiar laughter from across the room that has my head turning. As I see the source of the noise, whatever high I've been riding begins to diminish.

A dark-haired beauty dressed in white-wash jeans and a blue blouse has her arm looped through Owen's, and they're walking across the marble floor, laughing together while they carry on a conversation I can't hear.

Memories of walking in on Gavin fucking the blonde on my couch assault me, but I remind myself that Owen isn't my boyfriend. He isn't anything other than my fake fiancé and hotel roommate.

Though the ache in my chest says differently, I force myself to stay calm. This is what I asked for. I told Owen I wasn't going to offer him anything other than sex, and I never asked him to be exclusive.

I'm not allowed to be upset.

He finally sees me staring at them from my spot at

the coffee bar. His face pales for a second before he whispers something to the woman and walks away from her. She frowns, and something passes over her eyes when she sees me, but I don't stare at her for long. Owen is in front of me before I can decide what to do next, and I have no idea what to say.

"That isn't what it looked like," he says first, reaching a hand to cup my elbow.

I raise a brow and tilt my head. "It wasn't a beautiful woman garnering your attention?"

He sighs. "Yes, but there's more to the story that I didn't want to share with you, because it's complicated, but I'll tell you whatever you want to know. First, I need you to know I'm not interested in Natalie. She's only a friend from work that's caught up in this mess with Jack. I'm just trying to help."

"Okay."

"Okay? That's it? You don't have a million questions about what you saw?" A crease forms between his eyes. He doesn't like my lack of care, and I'm glad I stopped myself from allowing his actions to hurt me.

Protecting my heart in this way is exactly what I wanted to achieve. I'm not stubborn enough to deny that I like Owen for more than the killer sex we've been having—especially after the time we spent together this morning, getting to know each other better—but my ability to internalize my freak-out shows me that I'm able to keep a separation between us that will hopefully prevent myself from getting hurt once this fling ends.

"I just told you yesterday that whatever this is between us will only last until I get on the plane back home, Owen. If you say you were only helping a friend from work, then so be it. Even if she's interested in you, then it's whatever. I'm not going to make a big deal out of this."

He steps closer, and his eyes darken. "I would never want to hurt you, Ella."

I lick my lips and the walls around my heart shake, but I steel my resolve and smile. "I appreciate you saying that, but it's not necessary. I'm not hurt."

Owen pulls me into a hug. "I had plans of surprising you with a hike since our ziplining ended early thanks to Jack getting his junk pinched in the harness, but if you're not up for one now, I understand."

I can't help but laugh, especially since I'd love nothing more than to move on from whatever I just saw. "Please tell me you got a video of that."

Owen pulls back, but he keeps a hold on my hands. "Unfortunately, I left my phone in a locker so I didn't lose it while up in the air. My fear of heights had me overthinking a bit. I also won't deny that I was beyond okay with never making it past the 'baby runs' as the guide called them."

I pull a hand out of his grip and pat his shoulder. "You poor baby."

I've easily moved us beyond the moment with him and his co-worker, but that's more for my benefit than his. If I don't dwell on what I did or didn't see, then the actions don't have the power to hurt me.

Instead, I nod toward the door. "How about that hike, then? There was a beach I didn't make it to yesterday that I really wanted to check out. Maybe we can go there."

"Absolutely. Let's go change and we'll head out." His voice is confident, but the deep way he's staring into my eyes says something else. He doesn't believe that I'm fine, but I need him to...more for myself than anything else.

I force a smile up to my face before taking a step toward the elevators. "Okay."

He grimaces while we walk. "I don't like that word anymore."

I laugh. "Get over it, Okay Owen."

Chapter Seventeen

PEE ON YOU

Owen

Seeing Ella standing in the lobby when I was with Natalie, still putting on a show for Jack, gutted me. I should have told Ella that morning what was going on and why I might be hanging around another woman, but I chickened out.

Her not freaking out makes me feel worse. Not that I want to hurt her—that's the last thing I would want—but some anger would have been preferred over her shrugging things off. She didn't even ask any questions after agreeing to go on a walk to the beach with me.

The situation has me fucking baffled, which doesn't happen very often. I don't like the uncertainty of not being sure of where things stand between us. Not one damn bit.

We've been on the trails for two hours by the time we

finally get to the beach she failed to mention was miles from the resort.

Ella pulls on my hand. "Come on. We have to go this way before we get to the sand."

I follow her down a path that doesn't look used much. Probably because the hike back up to the trail is going to be a bitch. Though, the beach does look peaceful below and Ella seems too excited to try to warn her off continuing.

"You're slow," she teases before letting go of me and racing ahead.

I laugh and start to jog, so she doesn't get too far ahead. When we get to the bottom, white sands greet us and there isn't another soul in sight. The waves crash gently on the shore, and I'm ready to sit my ass down after all the walking we've been doing, but Ella has other plans.

She yanks off her cover-up dress and grins. "I want to swim."

I return the smile and pull my shirt off. "Then, let's go."

I'd opted to wear my jogging stuff instead of swim trunks when we were changing since I figured we'd be doing more hiking than swimming. I'm regretting that decision now, but the thin fabric of my shorts will dry quickly enough once we're out of the water.

By the time I have my shirt, socks, and shoes off, Ella's halfway to the water in a black bikini I haven't seen her wear yet. All of my favorite parts of her are covered, but it would take just a firm tug on the strings holding the fabric to her and she'd be on display for me.

When my feet touch the water, it's warm and comforting, but the relaxing moment is gone when Ella splashes me, soaking my face.

"You were looking a little hot," she says with a shrug.

She's been extra playful since we left the hotel. It has me on edge, wondering if maybe Ella's overcompensating to hide whatever she's really feeling.

Instead of asking her and ruining our time, I charge forward. "I was about to say the same about you."

I lift her up into the air and throw her farther into the low waves. She spits and sputters as she surfaces, but when her face clears of water, she's all smiles.

"Okay, Owen. I see how it's going to be." She continues to use "okay," and this version of Ella that likes to infuriate me is going to be punished.

She disappears under the water, but it's crystal clear and I give chase when she swims away from me.

Little white fish dart away from us when we disturb them, distracting Ella. I take the opportunity to catch up to her. My hands are around her waist and I'm lifting her out of the water once again, but this time I don't intend to let her go.

I lift her up, and she yelps. "I want to swim with the fish."

"That's not normally something people *want* to do," I say with a laugh.

She rolls her eyes. "You know what I mean. Now, you've scared them all away."

"I'm sure they'll be right back. In the meantime..." I dunk her below the water and quickly lift her back up.

Ella's fists are flying when she comes back up, and I narrowly miss getting punched in the eye. "No sexy time for you."

I palm her pussy. "That also means no dick for you."

Her eyes heat, and I know she regrets her choice in threat, but she's stubborn enough that she won't take the words back.

She opens her mouth, but an unexpected wave rolls through and takes both of our feet out from under us. I try to keep my hold on Ella, but she slips away.

Once the wave passes, we both resurface, and I release my tension when I see she's laughing. "Where the hell did that come from?"

"No clue, but looks like more are coming," I say. The water is rising and we're in its way. I reach a hand to Ella, but she's frozen.

"What's wrong? Did something bite you? I'll pee on you if I have to." I'm only half-joking, but she doesn't even crack a smile.

I look down in the water, but I don't see anything. "Ella?"

"My bottoms are gone," she whisper-yells.

"What?" At first, I have no clue what she's talking about, but then I realize she means her swimsuit bottoms. I duck under the surface and begin swimming around her, but there is nothing floating in the water except some of the fish who dared to return.

"I don't see them," I say when I come back up.

Her voice rises in pitch. "I only have my sheer cover-up, Owen. I can't go back to the hotel without my bottoms."

She's losing it, but I have an idea. "Come on. I'll fix this."

When I'm out of the water, I realize she hasn't followed me. I go over to the bushes and yank on the big palm leaves. "We'll cover you with these."

"You're out of your damn mind," she snaps, narrowing her eyes.

I'm totally kidding, but it's too good of a moment to pass on messing with her.

"Oh, I know. I can tie my shirt around you like a diaper. That should work perfectly," I add.

"Owen," she warns.

Her cheeks are growing redder by the second, so I decide to put her out of her misery. I take my jogging shorts off and my black boxer briefs with them. I put the shorts back on and dangle my briefs in front of me.

"You can wear these. Just roll them at the waist and put your cover-up back on. No one will be the wiser as long as we go right back to the room."

Her glare lessens, and she exits the water. "You're lucky you're cute."

"Hey, I just saved you from wearing leaves back to the resort. I should be sexy as hell."

She shrugs and tries to snatch the briefs from my hand. I hold on tighter and draw her toward me. "You know, since you're already half-naked and we're alone..."

She barks out a laugh. "Not a chance in fucking hell. I'm not getting sand anywhere near my vagina."

I release the briefs. "What if you could make a pearl from said sand?"

Ella flips me off and takes a few steps away from me.

I shrug. "Hey, you can't blame a guy for trying when he gets his eyes on that delectable pussy of yours."

She's fighting a grin while she yanks on the underwear. Instead of continuing to harass her, I grab her cover-up and slip it over her head once she's standing straight. "All better?"

"Thank you for being my knight in shining armor," she deadpans.

"You joke, but Prince Charming is my middle name," I tease.

"Uh huh, and my full name is Cinderella. Come on, *Prince*. Let's get back before I lose any more of my clothes."

I grab my shirt and slip my shoes on, then follow her back up the trail, enjoying the sway of her ass in my briefs while she hikes ahead.

Chapter Eighteen

LIKE A FUCKING ANGEL

Ella

We make it back to the hotel only to find Robert waiting for us. He's tense and avoiding eye contact. If Owen's room flooded, I'm going to kick someone's ass.

"I'm sorry to bother you, Mr. Porter, but I was told to make sure you got this message as soon as you returned. Mr. Harrington requires your presence tonight. He would like you to join him and some other employees during karaoke night."

"Thank you, Robert. I'll let Mr. Harrington know myself that I won't be able to make it," Owen says.

Robert grimaces. "I was also told that if you declined then I needed to tell you that this is non-negotiable. Failure to join your team for the night will be considered insubordination and possible termination may be considered."

Damn, Jack really has a hard-on for Owen. I still don't quite understand why he chooses to stay when there are so many other companies he could work for and still make a difference, but that's not really my business. I just want to get back to the room and feel more dressed.

Owen's jaw grinds together and he speaks through gritted teeth. "I'll join them as soon as I've showered and changed."

"Very well, Mr. Porter. They're on the tenth floor, in the night club," Robert says, and the relief in his tone is palpable. Jack must have scared the hell out of the poor guy.

Robert hurries off, and I follow Owen to the elevators. He scans his card aggressively, and I'm annoyed that our fun time—minus losing my swimsuit bottoms—has been ruined.

"At least he didn't require your presence at something boring like cheesemaking," I say to break the silence.

Owen snorts. "Cheesemaking?"

I shrug. "Been there, seen that. It's not all that fun."

"Right. Well, guess what? You're coming with me."

My head is shaking before he even finishes that sentence. "I don't think so. I want to punch Jack in his balls."

"Now *that* would be entertaining," Owen says.

"Seriously. I'm not coming with you." I cross my arms and take a step back.

Owen raises a brow. "Yes, you are."

"No and you can't make me."

"Who didn't want to bring any of their stuff with them on our walk? You have no phone or room key. The room is in my name. Unless you can track down Rosa, nobody is letting you in besides me. I'll leave you out here in my briefs all night unless you agree."

I narrow my eyes on him. "You wouldn't."

"Oh, I would." His smile is sexy as fuck, but I try to ignore the tightening in my stomach his grin evokes.

"You and Kenzie would make excellent friends. She enjoys threats by blackmail as well," I say.

"Then, I look forward to meeting her one day," he replies.

The one sentence has my internal walls creeping up. Owen won't be meeting Kenzie. He won't be meeting any of my friends once we're back home. I can't let this week of magical fucking go beyond the island. Especially not after what I saw before our hike.

His mouth downturns, but when he scrubs a hand over his face, the sullen look is gone. As the elevator doors open, he tosses me over his shoulder and carries me into the hallway, humming while he walks.

Before I can object, his palm smacks my ass. "What's it going to be, Ella? A night making fun of people by my side, or a night locked out of the room with all of your belongings just out of reach?"

"I don't like you," I grumble.

He laughs. "You don't have to like me to enjoy fucking me."

Wasn't that the truth, but I knew it was also a lie. Despite what did, or didn't, happen with Natalie, I do like Owen and his light personality and the way he always seems to know what I need. It's damn irritating, but attractive at the same time.

Owen opens the door to the room and sets me down just outside of the door, but he doesn't let go of my ribs. "Will you be joining me, Ella?"

I want to say no. I want to tell him to fuck off. I want to not feel something in my chest when I look into his blue eyes so full of life. I want a lot of things, but I'm realizing we don't often get what we want in this crazy thing called life.

"Fine, but I'm not going to like it," I reply with a childish pout.

His lips press against mine, taking me by surprise. The quick kisses feel more intimate than when he has his tongue shoved three inches down my throat.

Fuck. I don't like this.

At least, I don't want to.

———

AN HOUR LATER, WE'RE SITTING AT A TABLE IN the night club. I'm disappointed to find out that Jack has reserved the whole area for only his company. I was hoping to see the frisky old couple that we met in the elevator once I realized we were getting off on the same floor they had.

They could have made this night more bearable.

Owen leads us to a table, and the farther we walk into the room, the tighter his hold becomes on me.

"You don't have to stay if you don't want. I thought this might be fun, but maybe I was wrong," he says when the other employees stare. None of them have brought dates, and my presence hasn't gone unnoticed.

I try to avoid some of the looks, but there are so many glares and thinning of lips that they're hard to ignore.

"Yeah, maybe I should go," I say.

Before we can turn around, Jack approaches us. "Your concierge must not have relayed that this is a private event."

His dark gaze travels over me, and his upper lip lifts briefly before the jackass smirks. "But you're here now, so why don't the two of you join us at our table. I'll have another seat brought over."

Owen shakes his head. "That's okay, Jack. Ella wasn't going to stay. She just wanted to grab a drink from the bar, and then she was headed back up to her room."

I don't miss the way he says "her room" instead of ours.

Jack's predatory stare burns into me. "No, I insist she stays."

My stomach churns. I want to run for the door, but

it would give Jack too much pleasure to see that he's gotten under my skin.

Instead, I lift my chin and grin at him. "Thanks, Jack. I love karaoke."

Owen groans next to me, but there's nothing he can do. I'm staying, and I'm going to fuck with his boss as much as I can while I'm here because why the hell not.

"Fantastic. Follow me." Jack's posture is stiff, but his stride is swift while we trail behind him.

Owen leans closer to me and whispers, "You really don't have to do this."

I wink in return. "But I want to."

He groans. "This isn't going to end well."

"Probably not, but don't worry, I won't take things too far unless he forces me to," I say. Seeing Owen's unease, I decide I won't push Jack unless he pushes first. Okay, maybe I will a little, but not as obviously as I'd prefer.

When we get to the table, there's a seat next to the woman Owen called Natalie. I make an assumption, thinking Jack will place the extra chair there, but he doesn't. Instead, he sits it right next to his own.

"Have a seat," Jack says to me, then gestures to the rest of the table. "Everyone, this is Ella. She's Owen's *friend*. Ella, this is Todd, Mason, and Natalie."

I offer a smile and wave to the rest of the table. "Thanks for letting me crash your party."

Mason licks his lips. "You're welcome to crash *my* party anytime you want."

Owen stiffens as he takes his seat between the dirtbag and Natalie.

I give Mason a onceover. "I'm not sure you could handle me."

Todd chuckles, and Jack pats my head. "Now, Ella. I'm sure Mason didn't mean it like that."

I grip Jack's hand, letting my nails bite into his wrinkled skin just enough that he'll take notice and shove the meaty extremity away from me as he settles into his seat. "My apologies, then."

Natalie and Owen share a look I try not to notice while I scooch my chair further away from Jack. Todd begins to say something, but his words are drowned out when a woman's high-pitched voice echoes through the room.

My head turns to see karaoke night is in full swing, and not everyone brought their singing voice with them. Though, I don't judge. It takes guts to get up on stage and sing in front of people. Especially ones you work with.

She's belting lines to *Pocketful of Sunshine* and completely off key, but she knows the words and smiles brightly as she sways to the tune. At least she's having fun. I'd rather be her right now than myself.

Another minute later, she's done and bows, but only a third of the room claps for her. Though, she hobbles off the stage and doesn't seem to give a shit about the lack of reception she receives.

An announcer steps onto the stage. "Let's give Lisa

another round of applause. Next up, we have Frank Meyers."

An older man jumps onto the stage and snags the microphone. "Thanks, dude." Then, he turns to the crowd. "Let's party!"

Y.M.C.A comes on and I sigh. This guy enjoyed the seventies a little too much.

Jack leans across the table. "Owen, I forgot to tell you thank you for staying with Natalie yesterday and holding on to her while she was so sick on the yacht. I'm sure your touch really helped to keep her calm. Isn't that right, Natalie?"

Her eyes widen and her shoulders stiffen while Owen doesn't seem to react at all nor look at me. "I'm just glad I was sober enough to help. How are you feeling after the...incident earlier?"

Owen's question is asked casually, but makes Jack's mouth flatten. "Just fine."

Take that, asshole. Maybe Owen will do enough pushing of his boss's buttons that I can simply enjoy the evening.

I drum my fingers over the table. "I think I want to sing."

Todd scoffs. "This is for employees only."

Before I can reply, Jack is already getting up. "No, I think that's a great idea. Let me go get you on the list. You don't mind if I pick the song, right?" He raises a brow at me, and I don't back down from the challenge.

"Sure thing. Just stay away from the boy bands," I say

with a feigned shudder. I actually love those songs and hope my reverse psychology works on the prick.

He smirks, and the look doesn't fill me with anything positive.

Owen is eyeing me. His brows are drawn together and lips are pursed, but I ignore his concern. I can handle Jack.

"Where are you from, Ella?" Natalie asks before Jack returns. Maybe Owen wasn't lying. Maybe she doesn't want him the way it looked in the hotel lobby. Or maybe she's a really good actress. Either way, I'm not letting myself care.

"Born and raised just outside of Charlotte. I didn't realize that's where you all were from until today," I answer before reaching for an untouched glass of water in the middle of the table.

She smiles. "I wasn't raised in North Carolina, but I've been there a few years and have no plans of leaving."

Hmm, is she trying to say something else? Or am I reading too much into her words?

Before I can ask any of my own questions, Jack returns with a triumphant smile rising on his face. I try not to be worried, but I can't help wondering what he's up to.

The old guy is applauded off the stage and the announcer comes back to the stage. "We have a special addition to the lineup. Our first duet of the evening! Please, welcome Owen and Natalie to the stage."

Oh, that fucker. He isn't trying to humiliate me.

He's trying to remind me that I'm not the only one Owen has shown interest in since arriving in Saint Lucia. Hats off to him, because I didn't see that one coming.

Owen's jaw tenses. "I didn't agree to go up there, Jack. And neither did Natalie."

Jack smiles with an evil glint in his eye. "Natalie mentioned being too afraid to go up on the stage by herself before you got here. I thought maybe you'd want to help her out before Ella goes on. I signed all three of you up."

Everyone in the room except our table is clapping and cheering, oblivious to the tension bearing down on the five of us.

Natalie sways in her chair and falls into Mason. "I'm not feeling very well, Jack. I don't think I can get up there. My body still feels like it's on the yacht from yesterday."

Her skin pales, and she covers her mouth before gagging. If she's faking, she's one hell of an actress.

"Natalie? Owen? Where are you two lovebirds? We're ready for you," the announcer says, searching the crowd with a hand over his brow.

Owen stands and grins at me. "I guess Ella will have to fill in for Natalie since the song is already queued up."

Jack slides back roughly in his chair. "I'm sure they can swap the lineup to give Natalie a minute to feel better."

I pat Jack's shoulder with a smirk growing on my face. "That's okay. I'll go twice if I need to. Unless someone else would rather sing with Owen. I'm happy to give the spot up to any of you."

I glance at all three men. Mason and Todd don't meet my gaze, but Jack does while he reaches for his scotch.

He tips the glass toward me. "Have fun up there."

As I take a step away, he mutters something under his breath that's probably best I don't hear while I circle around the table to meet Owen.

When Owen and I are standing in front of the microphone, I peek down at the machine to find *Don't Go Breaking My Heart* as the song chosen. This would have been the last song I'd choose for a duet with Owen, but there's no time to ask for a change when I hear the melody start up. I would never give Jack the satisfaction of watching me bow out.

Owen gives my hand a squeeze. "Ready?"

I nod, and he leans toward the microphone first. I'm pleasantly surprised when his voice isn't terribly off key. Definitely deeper than Elton John, but at least I'm not cringing.

I move in next to him, so we can share the mic and sing the next line. My voice is scratchy, but nobody boos. Still, I attempt to clear my throat while Owen does his verse.

Both of our voices get better as we sing the words from the screen, and I don't realize until it's too late that Owen has his arm wrapped tightly around me. We turn toward each other while the lyrics leave our lips, and our gazes stay locked. The room fades away, and I can't see anything other than him.

Now that Owens's found his rhythm, I'm lost to his voice. It's like a fucking angel. Deep, but smooth and packed full of unspoken words. Words I don't want to hear or think.

I'm so distracted by him that I nearly miss my next line, but I belt the words off key just in time.

Owen doesn't miss a beat and his eyes never leave mine while we finish the song. I don't smile back. I hardly breathe. I don't know what to do. I probably look and sound like an idiot as a meltdown builds inside me, but I don't care one bit.

All I know is that as soon as the song finishes, I'm the first one off the stage. I don't wait for Owen. I don't go back to the table. I don't say another word.

I head straight for the door, and I'm grateful to look back and see Owen waylaid by Jack. I might have thought I won this round with him, but the tables turned, and Jack's triumphant grin tells me he's fully aware of his success, even if it hadn't come the way he planned.

I exit the club and, instead of heading to the beach or trying to convince Robert to give me another key, I head to the downstairs bar.

It's time to drown my thoughts.

Chapter Nineteen

A GOOD DICKING

Owen

I HAVE NO IDEA WHERE ELLA WENT, BUT I CAN'T sleep until I find her. I left the nightclub—much to Jack's dismay—and searched the beach, but she wasn't anywhere outside that I could see. I don't know what happened to make her run, but I need to find out.

I didn't expect Jack to try to interfere, but Ella handled him perfectly once again. I thought everything was going to be fine once we got up on that stage, but clearly, I missed something important.

After walking around for an hour, I head back inside the hotel. I hear shouts from the bar and ignore them until I hear the words "take it off" being chanted. I don't know why, but they give me instant dread.

I turn back around and go into the bar area. I find Ella dancing on the wooden counter to some pop song.

Her hands are gripping the bottom of her tank top, bringing it up and down. She's only showing off her stomach, but that's too much for me to handle.

Without thinking, I push through the growing crowd of men and grab Ella's legs. She doesn't see me coming and falls over my shoulder with an audible umph.

"Let me down," she screeches.

"Yeah, bro. Put the beautiful woman down," another man says, grabbing my arm.

I swirl around, careful to make sure I don't smack Ella's head on anything or anyone. "This is my fiancée. Now, get out of my way."

I haven't had to play the fake fiancé part much, and I'm happy to use it now. The other men hold their hands up and back away.

"I'm not yours," Ella gargles, dangling upside down.

"This sweet ass is mine until you leave this island, Ella. You don't get to shake it for those men in there without punishment."

I hear her sharp intake of breath, and she says nothing else. I make it to the elevator and don't bother to put her down when I scan my card and select the floor.

She wiggles over my shoulder. "I didn't do anything wrong."

"You're right, Ella."

"Why are you so mad, then?"

I make an odd noise. I don't really know how to answer her. I'm not mad. I'm frustrated. It's not Ella's fault that I let myself care for her and that the connection I'm trying desperately to hold on to only grew while we were up on the stage together.

"I'm not mad, Ella. I just don't like to share. We had a deal. You are mine until this vacation is over. Unless you're backing out of our deal, I'm taking you back to our room to remind you what it means to be mine."

"Fuck me," she whispers.

"Yes, I'll be doing that as well," I reply smugly.

The doors open to our floor, and I keep her propped over my shoulder until we're inside the room. She wiggles above me, and I bring her forward, catching her when she loses balance before placing her on her feet. She's wearing shorts, and they need to come off immediately.

I press her against the door and yank on the buttons. She stares at me with wild eyes and licks her lips. "Are you going to fuck me against this door again?"

"Is that what you want?" I ask, and she nods. "Then, that's what you'll get."

I get her undressed and pull my pants down far enough that I can get a condom on. The seconds it takes to sheathe my cock has Ella panting in my arms.

She might be drunk, but she still knows what she wants, and that's me. Me fucking her until she can't remember her own name. Not anybody else on this damned island. The truth of that thought returns some of my calm.

I lift her up, and she wraps her legs around my waist. I'm not gentle with her when I press her over my dick.

Her slick heat tightens around me, and I thrust in and out until her head pushes against the wooden door.

My right hand moves up her side, over her tits, and stops just under her chin. I wrap my fingers around her throat. The action gets her attention, but my touch is soft.

"I don't share, Ella," I remind her before driving into her again.

She nods. "I wasn't going to let them touch me."

"Only me, Ella."

"Only you," she says before rocking against me, then softly adds, "for this week."

Those last three words make me want to withdraw from her, but I don't. I move us from the door to the small table next to the kitchenette area. I lay her over the wooden surface and lift her legs up so that both of her ankles are next to my head.

My cock is still throbbing inside her, but I've stopped moving.

She looks up at me with hooded eyes. "Are you going to make me beg, Owen?"

I grip her hips tightly. "Tell me what you want, Ella."

"I want you to fuck me on this table until I scream your name," she says without hesitation.

I pull back enough to slam forward again, disappointed she didn't say she just wanted me.

Her ankles tighten around my ears, and she moans. "Just like that, Owen. Hard, fast, and dirty. Don't be gentle. Not tonight."

As much as I want her to tell me why she ran off and what has her so needy, I refrain, only doing as she asks. I fuck Ella on the table until she does just as she knows I like. She screams my name and begs me for more.

I can't find it within me to deny her, and my cock isn't done giving her a good dicking. I move us to the bedroom, intent to remind Ella just why she agreed to stay with me in the first place.

————

THE NEXT MORNING, I HAVE A MESSAGE ON MY phone from a number I don't recognize. One that asks me to meet them in the gym on the fourth floor.

Ella is still sleeping, and I take a moment to appreciate her natural beauty. I wish I knew what makes her so scared of what she's feeling, and worse, of what I feel. I might have agreed to her asinine plan of keeping our fucking only in Saint Lucia, but I already know I'm going to break that promise.

Another text comes through from the same number:
Five minutes.

I can't help my curiosity, so I decide to respond, hoping it's Bill and not Jack from a different phone.
Me: Be there soon.

Once I'm dressed, I kneel next to the bed and rub the back of my hand over Ella's arm. She grunts and the sound makes me smile.

"Good morning, gorgeous. I need to run downstairs

for a bit, but I want to talk about last night when I'm back. Don't go anywhere."

She grumbles something I don't understand, so I leave her a note just to be safe. She's probably not feeling all that well after whatever she drank in the bar.

As soon as I scribble the note and leave it next to her pillow, I race for the door, getting to the gym as quickly as I can. I walk in wearing loose shorts, my t-shirt from last night, and tennis shoes. I see four other men and a woman using various machines.

One of them turns toward where I stand in the door, and I notice it's Bill. He nods at the treadmill next to him and I take the cue. Even if by some crazy chance he's not the one who sent the messages, I don't want to offend him.

"Good morning, Owen," he says when I step on the machine.

"Morning, Bill."

I set my pace slow and begin a light jog.

"How has this week been going for you?" he asks.

"Honestly, the best parts have had nothing to do with the retreat," I answer.

He chuckles. "I saw the woman you were with last night. I'm surprised you left to follow her, even though Jack clearly ordered you not to."

I'm equally surprised that Bill was lurking in the club and none of us noticed him, but I don't say that. "If Jack wants to fire me, it won't make me sad in the slightest."

"Well, it would me. I need your help, Owen," Bill says quietly, confirming he's the one who texted.

"I assume this has to do with what Natalie found?" I ask.

He glances around and nods curtly. People are far enough away that they can't hear us with our low tones. "I need you to get access to Jack's computer and pull the accounting files he has on there for me. Put them on a flash drive. Once we have physical proof of what she stumbled upon, we can force him out."

Natalie couldn't confirm if Jack was embezzling money, but from what she described and with Bill wanting the accounting file, it sure the hell sounds like my initial assumption is right. Jack might have thought he got lucky when someone without a lot of corporate experience found the discrepancy, but he underestimated the meek personality of Natalie.

While I'd love nothing more than to see Jack get fired, I'm not an idiot and I don't want to go into this blindly. I need Bill to give me more information before I get too deep into some corporate espionage bullshit.

"Why me?" I ask.

Bill adjusts his speed down and checks around us again before lowering his voice even more. "I already had an interest in approaching you since you work so closely with Jack while in the office. Then, Natalie mentioned she was certain we could trust you. The board doesn't want to involve her more than necessary. She has no clue what she discovered, and the less people who know the better until we have the proof we need. We believe you could be the person we need to get that."

My pace slows on the treadmill. Everything he's saying lines up with what I'd been assuming before. Natalie was just in the wrong place at the wrong time, and now she's in over her head, but I wouldn't be if I agreed to help Bill.

"What exactly would you need from me?" I ask.

He swipes a towel over his face. "We need you to remain in Jack's good graces and get to his laptop sooner rather than later. We didn't think he'd be so concerned with me showing up here, but it raised more flags than the board was prepared for. We don't want Jack disposing of the evidence we need to fire him."

I've been pretending with Jack for a long time. I can placate him a while longer if it means getting him out of my life for the long term.

"I haven't been the most astute employee this week, but I'll see what I can do to make amends with him," I say.

Bill shuts down his machine completely and steps off. "We have all the paperwork in place already. You getting the proof we need to make sure Jack can't fight us in court over the termination is all we'll be waiting on to move forward. We're hoping to avoid any unnecessary scenes."

I stay on the treadmill and watch Bill exit the gym. With every step he takes, the churning in my gut intensifies. I know getting Jack out of the company is the right thing for everyone, but the longer I jog on the machine, the more I wonder if getting further involved in all this is the right choice.

Mostly, I'm worried I won't know if these niggling doubts are a warning I should have listened to until it's too late.

Chapter Twenty

HOTDOG DICK

Ella

OWEN IS GONE WHEN I WAKE. HE LEFT A VAGUE note but doesn't return before I've showered, so I decide to go for a morning walk. Today is my last full day in Saint Lucia. I miss my house and my friends, but it's been nice not worrying about work or Gavin too much.

Though, thoughts of Owen have turned from sexual to complicated. He fucked me senseless last night. It was once again exactly what I needed, but I haven't forgotten why I got drunk in the first place.

I have feelings for Owen, ones that will be hard to get rid of when I step onto the plane to go back home. The one thing I didn't want. Feelings mean he has the power to hurt me. That isn't sitting well inside my head, which tends to overthink things.

Once again, I find myself headed to the beach and avoiding the things that should be talked about.

I consider finding Rosa to ask her about some of the things she's already mentioned to me, but I can't find it within myself to do so. She'll ask how things are going, and even that simple question seems too complicated to answer at the moment.

There's a game of volleyball that appears to be starting soon. I'm tempted to ask them if I can join, even if it's just as an extra player, but before I do, I spot Blake.

He's kneeling next to a woman who's not his wife. The sight infuriates me. I know Cammie feels stuck and that Blake has her by the tits with her dad, but that doesn't mean I intend to stand by and let him treat her like shit.

Fury ignites within me as I waltz over to them, and I'm hovering over Blake.

"Tell me your room number and I'll meet you up there in an hour," he says, running a hand through his hair as if he doesn't have a care in the world.

The gorgeous blonde he's hitting on looks up at me instead of answering him. I wave and smile, letting the rage I feel for this disgusting man shine through my narrowed eyes.

"Can I help you?" she asks with a pinched expression.

"Actually, I think it's me who can help you," I say when Blake looks up.

"Ella," he warns, but I ignore him.

"You see, this man right here, he's married. In fact, he's on his honeymoon. Not only that, he likes to cheat on any woman he makes commitments to. If that fact doesn't deter you from his charms, this might."

I grab his wrist, first indicating to his hand, then his shoes. Blake is trying to talk over me, but I'm a force to be reckoned with this morning. "You'd think with these big hands and feet that the hotdog dick between his legs is more of a thick sausage, but I assure you, your vagina will only be disappointed by his weak hips once you fail to orgasm."

She lowers her sunglasses at me and smirks. "Thank you."

I move over just in time for her to grab a handful of sand and throw it in Blake's face. "Fuck off, hotdog dick."

He spits and sputters, wiping at his face, and I keep walking. Unfortunately, he catches up to me and grabs my arm painfully.

"What the fuck, Ella?"

"What the fuck, indeed," I say and yank out of his grip. "Cammie is a beautiful and smart woman. You, on the other hand, are a repulsive prick, and when I get home, I'm going to do everything in my power to ruin your reputation. Men like you don't deserve happiness and I hope your dick falls off from the next pussy it meets."

He gapes at me, and I storm off. Shit, that feels good. Cammie might be too afraid to go against her dad, but that won't stop me from following through on my threat to Blake. I still know some of his friends. I fully intend to put some extra bumps in the road for him when I'm home.

I don't know where I'm headed now, but I'm in a better mood. Maybe I will go find Rosa. I've still yet to try windsurfing. I think it just might be time I do that. On my own and just for me. Something to make me feel wild and alive.

———

THREE HOURS LATER, I'VE FINISHED MY tutorial in windsurfing. It sounds easy enough, and I've been wakeboarding. The boards look somewhat similar, which prevents me from psyching myself out.

My trainer and his buddy had a ten-minute conversation about which board to send me out with. That both confused me and made me feel better that they were putting that much thought into my safety.

As I straddle the 5.7 board with no clue why it's named that, I kick my feet to get myself into position. The wind, according to my trainer, is "on shore" which should be perfect for a beginner like myself.

Once I'm far enough out into the water, I do as I was instructed and take the uphaul in my hands before slowly standing up. My ankles wobble and knees shake, but the board is wide enough that I feel safe. Mostly.

I slide my feet into the designated spots and hold on

for dear life, hoping like hell the wind does its thing without killing me.

"Don't forget your right angle," the trainer calls from the beach.

Right. Angles. I need to pay attention to those to keep myself upright along with making sure my arms are straight, but knees stay slightly bent.

I'm absolutely out of my league with this whole windsurfing thing, but that's exactly why I'm out here. I want to do something just for me. Something new. Something to bring me a sense of wildness that isn't caused by anyone else.

I get myself into the proper position and finish pulling the sail all the way out of the water. I let out a massive sigh of relief when the sail goes into the right position instead of wayward like the trainer warned me could happen.

My hands grab tightly onto the mast and twist. I'm supposed to treat the mast and sail like a door. Opening it slightly so that the wind can come in and carry me along the waves. I don't really understand what that means, but when I feel a gust of wind on my face, I reach for the horizontal bar and give it a solid tug.

As I do, the board jolts forward and I'm moving over the water. I almost panic and release, but I manage to keep my grip firm. My speed picks up, and the faster I go, the more comfortable I get. I lean slightly back and relax my elbows when my pace levels out, and I can hear my trainer cheering for me from the shoreline.

A smile rises on my face, and I close my eyes for a moment to soak in the feeling of success. The invisible force that is the wind whips over me, but instead of letting myself be controlled by its strength, I'm commanding the powerful element.

When my eyes reopen, it's like I'm flying over the water. Birds soar above me. I'm one of them, moving with the waves, and nobody can stop me.

I'm on my own, and the magical euphoria filling me is like nothing I've ever experienced. I don't want to stop. I don't want to worry about going back to shore. I want to keep flying in the wind, enjoying the physical and emotional challenge I feel I've conquered.

The sun is warming my skin, and the water splashing around me is almost room temperature. I lean to one side and hold on tightly when the board goes over a wave, sending me a couple feet into the air. I come down hard on the water's surface. While my bones are rattled, I don't fall off and I let out a loud whoop.

This is exactly what I needed. The freedom to be on my own. To do something new. To just be. When the wind pulls me farther down the shoreline, I know then that no matter what happens, I'm going to be okay.

My exes can all fuck off. They no longer get to play a factor in my life choices. From this moment forward, I'm going to do exactly what I want, even if that means continuing to fuck Owen once I'm back in North Carolina.

That slice of happiness he's been offering? I deserve that, and I'm tired of denying myself joy.

———

"YOU'VE GOT TO BE FUCKING SHITTING ME?" I mutter to myself when I get back to the hotel. I had been riding one hell of a high since being on the water. Not even losing the feeling in my legs from standing so long on that board bothered me.

Now, though? All of that is dashed away when I see Owen. He's not alone and appears to be having the time of his life.

I left my phone in the room, so I haven't heard from him all day. I don't know why he's with Natalie this time, but I'm firmly set on the belief that she's a better actress than I thought. Owen said they were just friends, that he was only helping her with something that could get Jack fired, but I can't believe his words when his actions are smacking me in the face.

They're standing near the tables behind the coffee bar. Natalie's leaning her head against his shoulder and Owen's hand is gripping her hip while he's grinning down at her like she makes the sun rise in the mornings. He whispers something in her ear that makes her giggle, and the sound is more than I can handle.

I wasn't supposed to care. And just when I finally give myself the permission to do so, I see this? Fuck this bullshit. Fuck Owen. I should have known better. I shouldn't have fucking cared.

Though I have a fleeting thought to go punch him in the balls, I instead do something worse.

I leave with no intention of saying goodbye. Let that fucker sit and wonder what the hell happened to me. I couldn't give two shits if he worries. That's the least he deserves for making me a fool.

I'm in the elevator before they can see me. When I turn around to scan the key card, I see Rosa about to call for me, but I put a finger over my lips and shake my head. Her brows scrunch, but she stays quiet.

The doors close, and I ignore the burning in my eyes and the tightness in my throat. There are too many hours left before I need to be at the airport, and I can't be at this resort any longer.

I don't know where I'm going to stay, but I'm about to figure it out.

Chapter Twenty-One

WHAT THE SHIT

Owen

THIS HAS BEEN THE LONGEST DAY OF MY LIFE. Ella was gone from our room by the time I made it back, and she hadn't left a note like I did. I tried calling her only to find her phone on the table. I stayed as long as I could, in hopes she'd be back before I had to leave again, but I didn't see her before I headed to the morning gathering.

Jack is in better spirits today and has made my tasks easier. He thinks he ruined what I had with Ella thanks to his karaoke stunt, but I don't bother to tell him that she still did more than sleep in my bed last night.

Instead, I mentioned my interest in Natalie again. When Jack encouraged me to go to her, I didn't object. Though, I wanted to when he reminded me that getting closer to Natalie could mean big things for me. I'm not sure what Jack thinks will happen if I actually date Natalie, but I let him believe he's on to something instead of the other way around.

The day goes just as I hope. I convince Natalie to put on a brave face and stay close to Jack. The three of us and a few other department heads spend most of our time together, and my relationship with Jack is back to being as obediently superficial as it was before we got to Saint Lucia.

I'm waiting with Natalie in the lobby, and it's nearing dinner time. I need to get to the room and see if Ella's been back, but Jack asked us to wait for him.

"What do you think he wants?" Natalie asks me while I let her lean against me and keep my arm around her.

The action feels wrong, but the more I physically get close to Natalie, the happier Jack gets. Since she knows that this is nothing more than a show—especially after meeting Ella last night—I try not to let myself get too tense.

I glance down at her and smile. "I have no idea, but we'll find out soon and then you can go back to your room. I'm going to try and get invited to Jack's for dinner."

I haven't told Natalie that I need information from Jack's laptop. She doesn't need to be involved more than she already is, like Bill said, but I don't want her to feel in the dark either.

She lifts her hand and rests it over my chest while leaning closer. "You don't need my help with that?"

A shudder ripples through me at the contact, and I try not to grimace. "No, Jack won't open up with you around. It's better if I'm by myself."

"I can't say I'm disappointed by that fact," she whispers.

"Owen, come on over here," Jack's voice booms from the coffee bar.

My eyes cast down to Natalie. "Looks like you're off the hook already. I'll see you later."

Her smile widens, and she pats my chest. "Have fun."

Fun. Right. Not likely.

I waltz over to Jack with a grin on my face and reach for a mug. "Hey, Jack."

He's standing there, stirring too much sugar into his drink. "I thought after watching you run after that girl that Natalie didn't have a chance in hell with you, but, in this instance, it's nice to be wrong."

I turn to watch Natalie waiting at the elevators. "Ella was fun, but I only wanted one thing from her and I got it."

When I'm facing Jack again, he's grinning. "I'm glad to hear that. You see, Natalie has some leverage against me, and I need some over her. Maybe some pictures that could be rather embarrassing should they get out, if you know what I mean?"

He has to be fucking joking. I know he's not, but damn, I wish he was.

"I know what you mean. I don't think I can make that happen here, but once we're home, I'll do my best to get something for you quickly," I say, distracting myself with the coffee machine as I speak to hide the disgust on my face.

Jack clasps a hand over my shoulder. "I knew I could count on you. I have a dinner date, but if you're not busy tonight, come by my room and we'll share a drink while we talk about some more things that are long overdue in regard to your role at Harrington Enterprises."

I bite my cheek to keep from rolling my eyes or saying something that I shouldn't. There is no amount of money in the world that could ever convince me to treat a female with such disrespect, but I manage to nod and force a smile to my face to keep up the farce.

"I'll reach out when I'm free and you can come over," he says.

I busy myself with my coffee so I still don't have to verbally respond. He gives my arm another pat before heading for the elevators.

I shake my shoulders once he's gone and finish most of my coffee in a few gulps before setting the cup on the tray at the end of the counter.

I need to get back to the room and find Ella. I haven't seen her between events today, and she hasn't responded to any of my messages, which likely means she never went back to get her phone.

The sinking feeling in my stomach I had earlier hasn't left me all day, and I think that's because I haven't told Ella everything about Natalie. Ella hadn't asked when I gave her the opening, but I shouldn't have used that as an excuse to stay quiet. I shouldn't have been a coward about the situation.

I want to find her, grab dinner, and tell her everything, because the last thing I want is for her to think I've purposely lied.

When I get to the room, everything is quiet and my chest aches. I head to the bedroom, hoping to find Ella there, but the bed is empty. I look further and notice her bag that was on the chair this morning is no longer there.

Stepping into the bathroom, I find her toothbrush is gone as well. I open the drawers and only see my belongings within them.

"What the fuck?" I mutter.

I grab my phone and call her. No ringing, only straight to voicemail.

My breath comes in shallow gasps while I leave her a voicemail. "Ella, it's Owen. What happened? Where are you? Please call me as soon as you get this."

I call Robert next. "Hello, Mr. Porter. How can I help you?"

"Have you seen Ella Danes?" I ask.

"No, sir, I haven't. Would you like me to put you on hold and ask Rosa?"

"Yes," I say a little too harshly.

The line goes quiet, and I wait for what feels like forever.

"Rosa states she saw Ms. Danes getting into a taxi with her bag not too long ago, Sir."

My hand tightens around the phone, and the other turns into a fist at my side. "But her flight isn't until tomorrow late morning."

"Yes, that's correct."

I end the call with an abrupt goodbye. I have to find her. She must have gone to another hotel to wait out her departure time. Only I don't understand why.

Then it occurs to me. Ella could have seen me with Natalie while we were waiting for Jack. It wasn't like we were groping each other, but holding Natalie like I had been wouldn't have seemed innocent to Ella, given I'd failed to man up and tell her the whole situation sooner. Not after all she's been through.

"Fuck!" I shout to the empty room.

I don't know how I'm going to find Ella, but I'll be at the airport well before her flight tomorrow if I can't find her in any of the hotels. I'm not letting her leave this island without knowing the truth. Even if she doesn't believe my words, I know I need to do everything I can to make this right.

If I don't, the regret just might drown me.

Chapter Twenty-Two

I'M READY

Ella

MY FIRST PLAN WAS TO GO FIND A NEW HOTEL and hang out until morning, but I don't trust myself. If Owen searches for me and finds me, I'll be tempted to hear him out, and I don't want to. I can't stand the thought of being lied to. I know what I saw, and I won't be convinced of anything else.

To avoid that happening, I go straight to the airport and cry a little when I pay nearly a thousand dollars for a flight that doesn't even get me home today. No, this one goes to Philadelphia, where I'll sleep in the airport—or more likely, sit rigid in my seat until dawn—before my flight back to Charlotte departs at the ass crack of dawn.

But it's better than staying in Saint Lucia and dealing with the shitshow I've gotten myself into. At least, that's what I keep telling myself.

I try to think of the positives as I move through security. At least this time there isn't a dildo in my carry on. Though, I wouldn't be sad if I somehow got upgraded to first class again.

I manage to survive going through the metal detector and having my bag checked by security with only five minutes to spare before boarding begins. As much as I want to grab some snacks for the five-hour flight, I head straight to my gate. I'll have plenty of time for food when I'm sitting in Philadelphia all night.

When I arrive, they've already begun calling first class, and I don't see my name on the screen. I guess it's an aisle seat just a few rows from the bathroom for me. Whatever. At least I'm getting home without any further drama.

It's Thursday, and I don't have to be back at work until Monday. I intend to spend my flight finding something else for me to do on my own. Windsurfing had been just what I needed. Only, it hadn't given me the clarity I should have been looking for.

I made a mistake when I thought it was a good idea to take things further with Owen. Seeing him with Natalie reminded me why I should have stuck to my plans and spent these last few days by myself.

Maybe another adrenaline rush will point me in the direction of self-discovery. Maybe it will only end with broken bones. I don't know, but I'm ready to find out.

Chapter Twenty-Three

NOT DONE

Owen

IT'S GETTING DARK, AND I STILL HAVEN'T FOUND Ella. I don't know what I'm supposed to do. Her phone is off. She hasn't contacted the resort that I know of, and none of the other hotels have her as a guest. At least, not under the name Ella Danes.

The only other plan I have is to go back to my room and wait for her to either show up or head to the airport before I know she's due to fly out.

The idea of just waiting is driving me crazy. I want to be doing something, but there's nothing left to do that I can think of. That alone makes me feel more helpless than I have in a long time.

I get back to the hotel and head straight to my room, only to find Jack waiting at my door. As much as I want to help Bill, I'm all out of fucks to give. I can't be the inside man for the board. I can't work for Jack anymore. I can't pretend to give two shits about another woman when all I want is Ella.

Jack's typing on his phone before he looks up at me with narrowed eyes. "I saw Natalie getting food by herself. If you weren't with her, why weren't you answering my calls?"

I take a deep breath and consider what I'm about to do. I'm so close to getting Jack out of the picture. So close to helping make a difference in a company I know is capable of doing good. Yet, regardless of those things, I can't stop the words from spewing out of my mouth.

"Get the fuck out of my way, Jack."

The line between his brows deepens. "What did you just say to me?"

I sigh. "I don't have time to placate you anymore. I'm not going to help you get leverage over Natalie. In fact, I don't even want to work for you anymore. I'm done, Jack. With everything that has to do with you and your company."

His lips thin, and he takes a step closer. "Do you understand what you're doing right now? I will ruin you, Owen. You'll never work for another worthy company again."

I let out a dark chuckle. "Any company who trusts whatever you have to say about me isn't one I want to work for."

"You're going to pay for this." He steps forward, slamming his shoulder into mine before heading toward his room.

A weight is lifted off my chest the moment I unlock the door to my hotel room. Damn, I should have done that a long time ago. Then again, if I had, I wouldn't have been in Saint Lucia and might not have met Ella. I know I'm here for a reason, and I need to make things right. I was meant to be on that plane with her. I feel that in my soul.

With renewed determination, I head for the bedroom, looking for anything I might have missed earlier that could tell me where Ella went.

I open all of the drawers, then I strip the bed, and the bathroom gets the same treatment, but still, there's nothing left of the woman I'm not ready to let go of.

My phone rings and I hurry to pull it from my pocket only to find Natalie's name on the screen instead of Ella's. I consider sending her to voicemail, but she deserves to know what I've done.

"Hey, Natalie," I say.

"Is everything okay?" Her voice is softer than normal.

I sigh. "No. You'll need to get in touch with Bill. I got into it with Jack and quit. I won't be able to help the two of you. I'm sorry."

She's quiet for several seconds, and I look at the screen to check if she's hung up.

"I understand, Owen. Thank you for trying."

Before I can say "you're welcome," she's ended the call. Instead of tucking my phone away again, I send a text to Bill. I still want him to get the information he needs and don't want him to be blindsided by me quitting.

His response is immediate. ***Don't worry. We have a plan B. I'll be in touch.***

I'm not sure why he'd be in touch with me, but I won't be holding my breath waiting. Getting Ella back is my only priority, and that's where I let my thoughts get back to.

If she's not at the hotels, then where would she have gone? The answer eludes me, and I decide to get online. There has to be something on social media that can help me.

A quick search of her name and Charlotte, North Carolina together gives me a social media profile. It's not public, but I can see her friends list. At this point, Ella is either ignoring me or something has happened to her, which I'm trying not to consider as a possibility.

Whatever it is, I can work with what I've found. Ella mentioned something about her friend Kenzie and I being alike, so I search for her name in the friends list.

"Bingo," I say and click on the profile. I type out a message to her and hope she doesn't ignore me.

This is Owen, the guy Ella has been staying with. She left without saying anything. Have you heard from her? I just want to make sure she's okay.

Hopefully my words will appeal to the friend. If Ella is merely ignoring me, then I assume her friends will know, but if Ella's not snubbing me and something happened, they need to know as well.

I wait a few minutes, but my message isn't read. It's nearing seven in the evening. I don't know what else to do, but there has to be something.

A knock sounds at my door. I rush to open it, hoping to see Ella on the other side, but instead I'm greeted with Robert's grim face.

"Good evening, Mr. Porter. I have news on Ms. Danes," he says.

"And?" I reply when he doesn't elaborate.

"She flew back home this evening."

My grip on the door tightens, and my other hand flexes at my side. I can't believe she left without saying goodbye. She had to have seen me with Natalie, or Jack said something to her, or who the hell knows. No matter the reason, I'm not done with Ella Danes.

"Thank you, Robert. Can you please get me on the first flight out tomorrow?"

He nods. "Of course, sir. I'll bring you the itinerary within the hour."

I close the door and go back to check my phone. Kenzie still hasn't responded. I consider messaging the other friend Piper but decide to wait.

A plan is already forming in my mind. I don't know if Ella will believe me, but I know she feels something for me, and I can't let her walk away without a fight.

Not when she's the first woman who has made my chest ache and heart soar at the same time.

I'm coming for you, Ella Danes.

Chapter Twenty-Four

A FUCKING GODDESS

Ella

WHEN I WALK INSIDE MY HOUSE, I WANT TO crash onto the carpeted floor and sleep for a week. I didn't realize an overnight layover would kick my ass so severely, but I'm wasted.

I intend to take a nap, then pack for the hike I have planned for tomorrow morning, but when I get to the kitchen, I'm greeted by the glaring faces of my two best friends.

"Hello, there," I say with an awkward wave.

"Hello, there? That's what you have to say for yourself after turning off your phone and leaving us to think God-knows-what happened to you?" Kenzie practically yells.

"I'm sorry. It's just that—"

Piper cuts me off. "Nope. Sorry isn't going to fix this.

We spent hours calling the hotel and the airlines and the hospitals. We had no idea where you were or if anything had happened to you. We even tried the police, but nobody would help us until more time had passed."

Kenzie nods. "What she said. I just got done leaving a message for Owen through Harrington Enterprises. My boss is pissed because I didn't come into work this morning. I was seconds from calling the National Guard. So, Ella Danes. What in the actual fuck happened?"

I'm not sure how to answer her question. They have every right to be mad, but I did what I needed to do for me. Selfishly, I wasn't thinking about anyone else the moment I saw Owen with Natalie. I just needed to get away.

Get away from the feelings I'd stupidly let in. Get away from Owen before he could convince me he isn't like all the other men in my past. Get away from Saint Lucia.

"El, come on. It's us. You can tell us anything," Piper says.

I sigh and take a seat at the counter next to them. "I know, but I don't have a clear answer. I just ran instead of handling things like a grown-ass woman."

"Ran from what? Do I need to plot a murder that can be ruled an accident?" Kenzie asks and doesn't crack a smile. I know she's joking, but I love her even more for her efforts to cheer me up.

"I was starting to like Owen," I admit.

Piper lays her hand over mine. "Well, did you expect anything else once you started screwing him?"

I shrug. "I thought I could keep it simple."

"Life is never simple, babe. What made you run?" Piper asks.

"I saw Owen with one of his co-workers and not for the first time. He swore she was just a friend from work that needed help. I believed him at first, but seeing them together a second time was different. He didn't know I was there. The way he held her and how they looked at each other and just... Gah!"

Merely remembering what I saw in the hotel lobby has me flustered. I wasn't supposed to care enough about him to get this way. I was supposed to be done with men. I only wanted to fall in love with *myself* all over again. Not dive headfirst into a pool of emotions for another man.

"Playing devil's advocate here, so don't stab me. Did you stay long enough to ask him what was going on?" Kenzie asks.

I shake my head.

She brushes strands of her ginger hair back. "Then, maybe it isn't what you thought."

"No, you weren't there. I know what I saw. There was no point in waiting around any longer."

My hands rub over my face, and I hear one of the other stools scrape across the tile floor, then my fridge opens. Glasses clink together and settle on the counter.

A warm hand settles over my back, and I peek

through my fingers to see Kenzie smiling at me. "Everything's going to be okay, El. What you need right now is a mimosa, because, you know, it's not even lunch time. Then a nap, and later today, things will look a fuck ton better."

I crack my first smile since yesterday. "A fuck ton?"

"Maybe just half a fuck, but if you find a way to think of Owen as just a good screw, then he'll be easier to forget."

I chuckle. "He wasn't a good screw. He was an excellent screw."

Piper nudges me with her shoulder. "Then, you'll have even better memories, but the important part is that's what you think of them as now. Owen was someone who made your vacation not as boring as it could have been. Nothing more, nothing less."

I nod. I want to believe her, but my heart constricting the way it is at the mere thought of considering my time with Owen only as a memory tells me I'm a long way from thinking how they're suggesting.

"How about the three of us go do something fun this weekend? You don't have to go back to work until Monday, right?" Kenzie asks.

"Yeah, and as much as I love both of you, I'm going to do some things on my own," I reply.

Kenzie waggles her brows. "*Alone* alone? Or alone with you and B.O.B.?"

I lightly shove her back with a laugh. "Thanks to you, I'm missing a B.O.B. from my collection."

She straightens her shoulders and stands tall. "Oh, how I wish I'd been there. I was going to wait in the airport, but I thought you'd find that too suspicious if we didn't just drop you off. Tell me, was the TSA agent at least hot?"

"I hate you so much right now," I grumble while fighting off a smile.

Kenzie winks. "There's a fine line between love and hate, my gorgeous friend."

She's right, and I couldn't hate her even if I wanted to. Not her or Piper. They're my people. My forever friends. My sisters from other misters. The only two people in this world I know I can count on, which is why I need to kick them out of my house.

I grab each of their hands and smile. "I'm so thankful for both of you, but you need to leave."

Piper squeezes my hand back and smiles knowingly. Kenzie scoffs and glares. "Why the hell do we need to do that?"

"Ella has some things she needs to do," Piper answers for me.

Kenzie backs out of reach from Piper's outstretched hand. "Like what?"

I look each of them in the eye. "Like figuring out how to love myself as much as I love the two of you."

"Fuck," Kenzie mutters, and her eyes brim with unshed tears. She grabs on to my shoulders, meeting my gaze. "You are a fucking goddess. You are perfect in every way. Your smile lights up a dark room. Your heart is depthless and too good for this world. You are sexy as fuck, and your ass is to die for. Seriously, those cheeks are like chef's kiss. I believe in everything that you are, and I can't wait for you to see yourself the way we do. I'm so damn proud of you for taking this first step and doing this on your own."

I can't hold back my tears while I listen to Kenzie's speech. I wrap my arms around her, and Piper joins in. We're a tangled mess of tears, laughter, and hugs, and I wouldn't have it any other way.

"I don't know what I'd do without you two," I murmur.

"You'd be really bored," Piper says.

I laugh and wipe my cheeks. "Truth."

"Alright, we're going to go, but Monday night there will be dinner with the three of us, so you can tell us how your weekend of solitude goes," Kenzie says.

"Absolutely. I love you both," I reply, wiping my cheeks dry.

Piper gives me another hug. "We love you, too. More than all the stars in the sky."

"More than all the dicks on Earth," Kenzie corrects, making all three of us laugh again.

I nudge both of them toward my front door. "Okay, enough. I need to shower and sleep and finalize my plans for the weekend."

"You've got this, El," Piper says before they leave, and I believe her.

My self-love might have been damaged from the

relationships of my past, but I'm not broken. I can sense who I'm supposed to be buried deep beneath all the garbage. It's just going to take time to unburden myself from the shit I let other people make me believe was my problem.

It's time to be Ella Danes the way I have always wanted to be and forget about the version I think other people expect of me.

Chapter Twenty-Five

ANOTHER DICKASS

Owen

ELLA'S FRIEND KENZIE HAS YET TO READ MY message, and I've run out of options to reach Ella, which is how I've ended up at the airport. I'm not letting her get away easily. I may have only known her four days, but she makes my heart want to explode, and I'm not stupid enough to let her walk away from me.

Not unless that's truly what she wants.

I need to consider that as a possibility, but I don't like to live life with what-ifs. I refuse to let Ella be one. I'm going to find her, and I'm going to make sure she knows the truth. If she still doesn't want anything to do with me, I'll respect that choice, but only once I've explained what I'm beginning to believe she saw.

"Calling all passengers for Flight 652 to Charlotte.

We are now boarding all rows," a woman's voice sounds over the speaker.

I grab my carry-on and head toward the line forming. Thanks to my last-minute flight changes, I'm stuck in the back row, but I don't care. I just want to find Ella.

Even though I'm sure she's not here, I search around again for any sign of her, but no such luck. With a sigh, I hold my phone out and let the flight attendant scan my electronic ticket.

"Enjoy your flight, Mr. Porter," she says before following me to close the door.

Little chance of that, I think, but I also remind myself that if I can find Ella, then taking a cramped seat on a full plane will be the best thing I ever did.

Only when I finally get to my seat and see I've been seated next to a woman with a toddler too big to be sitting on her lap and stare into his devious eyes, I know it's going to be the longest five hours of my life.

———

I HAVE PERMANENT MARKER ON MY CHEEK, applesauce on my crotch, and something sticky embedded in my hair. Never before have I met a child so conniving, and I'm convinced the one next to me was touched by the devil when he was born.

His mother apologized several dozen times, but her words don't erase the black lines from my face or clean the crusty applesauce from the zipper of my jeans.

When the plane comes to a full stop, I look over at the toddler and want to scream when I see that he's finally asleep.

The mom just shrugs. Instead of being angry, I smile and step over her. I grab my carry-on from the overhead storage compartment and nearly kiss the flight attendant when he announces that they'll be allowing passengers to exit from the rear of the plane as well.

At least something is finally going right for me.

When I turn my phone off airplane mode, disappointment fills me that I still haven't heard from Ella or her friend. Though, I did as much cyberstalking as I could during the flight when I wasn't dodging the toddler's attempts to disfigure me and came up with a plan.

A deep dive into Kenzie's social media proved useful. She's almost too relaxed with the information she posts online. She works for a tech company, and I'm hopeful I can catch her before she leaves for the day. So long as they don't cut out right at five.

I make my way through the airport, annoyed about waiting nearly thirty minutes for my checked bag to come around the luggage carousel. At least I left my car in long term parking, so I don't have to depend on a taxi or car service.

It's 4:45pm, and if I don't run into any other issues I should get to Kenzie's work within the half-hour.

My stomach churns when I think of all the ways this

could end badly, but I know I have to try. Ella Danes needs to know exactly how she makes me feel.

―――――

NEARLY AN HOUR LATER, MY KNUCKLES ARE white and I'm pretty sure my steering wheel is dented. I got stuck on the interstate, thanks to a small accident in a section of the road where there is no place to pull off onto a shoulder.

With one-lane traffic backed up three miles, I'm certain I've missed my chance to find Kenzie before she leaves for the weekend. Regardless of my lost hope, I still head to the corporate office address I found online.

They only have one employee parking lot that I can see and it's about half-full. I park at the front where I can see a few doors I assume to be the ones that the employees use to come and go.

While I wait, I pull up Kenzie's profile again and get a fresh look at her face, so I don't accidentally approach the wrong woman and get the cops called on me.

Kenzie has deep auburn hair and light hazel eyes with fair skin that is free of freckles, at least from the pictures I've seen online. She shouldn't be hard to miss, but I won't be making any assumptions. Not when there is so much on the line.

Twenty minutes go by, and I've seen a couple dozen people leave, but none of them matching Kenzie's description. There are still another fifteen or so cars left, giving me a little bit of hope.

I wait another ten minutes and my efforts are rewarded. A redhead with her hair piled on top of her head and wearing a blue dress exits.

She has a phone up to her ear and looks concerned while she walks at a quickened pace toward the parking lot.

I hurriedly get out of my car and jog to make sure she spots me first. I don't want to scare her.

She grins. "Hey, Pipe. Let me call you right back." When she hangs up the phone, her eyes roam shamelessly over my tall frame. "Hello, handsome. How can I do you...I mean help you?"

Her words are more forward than I expect, but they also take away some of my nerves. "I'm Owen. I met El —" I'm cut off by Kenzie poking a finger in my chest.

"You have some nerve showing up at my work," she sneers.

I put my hands up in surrender. "I know what Ella saw, but I need to explain."

"No, what you need to do is stay the hell away from her. Ella's been through enough. She doesn't need another dickass in her life causing more turmoil," Kenzie says, stepping back from me and crossing her arms.

"If I'm right and Ella saw me with my co-worker Natalie, then it isn't what she thinks. I just want to explain and if Ella still hates me, then I'll leave her alone. I promise. Hurting her is the last thing I want."

Kenzie glares at me. "What is it that she saw?"

I'm surprised to hear Ella hasn't told them everything, but also concerned that I hurt Ella worse than I thought if she's keeping things to herself.

Since I don't know how much Kenzie knows, I do my best to make a long story short.

"Ella saw me once with this woman I work with, but I never fully explained who Natalie was and what I was doing. I assume Ella saw me with Natalie again and made a rightful assumption in the moment, but what I need Ella to know is that regardless of what I could have had with Harrington Enterprises, I walked away from the company as soon as I knew Ella was gone. That job means nothing to me if I have to hurt people I care about in the meantime."

Kenzie's arms are still crossed, and she's tapping her heel on the asphalt. Her poker face is solid, and I have no idea if she believes me, but I'm not going anywhere until I've exhausted every option in finding Ella.

"Why are you here?" Kenzie asks with an even tone.

I sigh, thankful she doesn't tell me to fuck off.

"Because I want to make sure Ella knows the truth before she decides to never speak to me again. She deserves better than what she thinks I did to her. I promised I'd never hurt her like that Blake guy did or any of her other exes, and I don't want her to think that's exactly what I've done."

Kenzie drums her fingers over crossed arms while

staring at me with thinned lips, but I don't shrink away from her intimidation.

"Ella's my best friend. The sister I never had. Her and Piper mean everything to me. The only reason I haven't killed Ella's exes for the way they've treated her is because the thought of being arrested for murder instead of having girls' night isn't all that appealing."

I fight a smile, because I don't actually think she's joking. Not entirely, anyway. "Understandable, but I promise not to give you a reason to plot my death."

Kenzie smirks. "Oh, the plotting is already done. Don't you worry there."

I want to return her smile but think better of it. "Well, that's...good to know."

She looks around and finally uncrosses her arms to pull up something on her phone, which reminds me that she never responded to my online message.

"I sent you a message through social media," I add while she's typing.

Kenzie shudders. "I never use messenger. Too many dick pics that I can't unsee." She hands me her phone. "Put your phone number in here. That's the only way you'll hear from me. When I think Ella is ready to see you, I'll call you."

"But if she doesn't know the truth then she might not ever be ready to see me," I say.

"You let me worry about that. For right now, all you get to know is that she has plans and I won't let you interfere with them. If I find out that you've tried to contact her again or show up anywhere that she might be, then you'll be seeing me a whole lot sooner than I guarantee you'll like."

I take Kenzie's threat seriously. I grew up with two sisters. I know how women like to flock together and how sharp their claws can be.

"Do you believe me that I didn't mean to hurt Ella?" I ask while I put my information in her phone, then send a quick text to myself so I have Kenzie's number as well.

She doesn't answer until I've handed her the phone back. "I'll admit, I did my fair share of looking into you and I haven't found anything glaring *yet*. Though, that doesn't mean I believe you."

I'm not sure how to respond to that, so I merely nod and take a step back. "Well, I appreciate you even considering letting Ella know I'd like to talk to her."

"I'm sure you do. If you can leave her alone for the weekend, I might be in touch." Kenzie slides her phone into her purse and walks away.

I watch her for a moment before going back to my car. I'm not sure our interaction went well, and the thought of not trying to reach Ella for another three days is already painful, but I'm going to try.

Unfortunately, I think Kenzie is my best chance at speaking to Ella. I have no choice but to hope Kenzie is merciful and doesn't make me wait too long.

Chapter Twenty-Six

GOOD FUCKING RIDDANCE

Ella

THE NEXT MORNING, I FINALLY TURN MY PHONE back on. I cringe at the plethora of messages from Piper and Kenzie, then do my best to ignore everything from Owen. Though, I can't manage to stop myself from reading his most recent message showing in the preview.

Owen: Please just let me know you're okay and I'll leave you alone if that's what you want.

Given I can barely tolerate reading that message, I know I won't survive seeing the others. I move on to let Kenzie and Piper know that I'm going for a hike and won't have my phone on, but it will be charged in case I run into trouble.

Piper: Be safe and remember we love you.
Kenzie: Say hi to Yogi bear for me!

I smile at their replies and turn my phone off again. I

already know where I'm going, so I won't need the GPS. My backpack is loaded with water and food to last me a full day, though I haven't decided if I'll stay overnight like I originally wanted. It's still a little too cold at night for sleeping under the stars.

After double-checking that I have everything I might need, I head for my car. Getting in the driver's seat feels weird, because I haven't driven since before my vacation.

When the engine turns over on the first try, I let out a sigh of relief that the battery hadn't died while sitting idle. I press the garage door opener and then shift into reverse.

As I back out of the driveway, I spot a familiar truck coming down the street, one I have no desire to see.

Gavin is slowing down and waving at me, but I pretend not to see him and hit the gas. My car jerks into the street, facing the opposite way I need to go, but also away from Gavin.

I press the garage door button again, praying it closes. I don't have time to stick around and make sure. Gavin is getting closer, and I don't want to talk to him. Yes, I'm running from my problems—again—but I just want this weekend to myself. I don't think that's too much to ask before I'm forced to go back to work and deal with real life on Monday.

My speed is much too high for the residential area, but with a few quick turns, I'm hopeful I lost Gavin and slow down. I send up a silent thanks that he hadn't arrived just a minute sooner.

Instinctively, I reach for my phone to call Kenzie or Piper, but then I remember I turned everything off for a reason. I need to look within myself and figure out who I am and what I want without outside influence.

Maybe that's the wrong choice, but my heart says it's what I need, and I'm doing my best to listen.

A few more glances in my rearview mirror and I'm relieved not to see Gavin's truck behind me or on the main road when I get out of the residential area. I continue to head east and away from the congestion of the city life.

With any luck, by the end of the day, I'll have gotten in a good workout, let go of a lot of tears, and enjoyed all the things nature has to offer.

———

I'M CRYING FROM LAUGHING SO HARD BY THE time I get back to my car at the base of the trail, my arms, face, and clothes are covered in dirt. My jeans have holes in them that didn't come from the designer, and I'm probably bruised to shit, but none of that is bothering me.

It's dark and windy and I'm pretty sure it's going to rain any minute, even though the weather I checked this morning said clear skies for the whole weekend. I'm not even sure what time it is, and even though I've been gone all day, a part of me isn't ready to leave.

I took the trails less traveled today. I got lost more

times than I care to count. I crossed paths with other hikers who probably think I escaped from a hospital. Most of them had to have heard me crying and screaming and laughing at some point. When my emotions weren't on a roller coaster, I stopped and napped under a tree just because I could, but then regretted that decision a short time later when I woke up covered in ants.

The ants wouldn't have been so bad except I might have freaked out more than necessary when I realized what was crawling on me and flailed around a little too much, which resulted in me tumbling down a hill.

I wish I could say that was where most of the dirt covering me came from, but that would be a lie. After the ant incident, I continued my hike instead of giving up and made it to the top of the hill where I spotted the most beautiful field of poppies growing.

Me being the new me and wanting to enjoy all the things, I ventured into the acre of colorful growth only to accidentally disrupt some sort of wasp or hornet hangout. I was only stung twice, but that was because I ran really fucking fast away from that field and took one last roll.

That time, it was down the trail that's incline should have killed me, but somehow, the worst injury I have is my pride. Though, as I lean against my car, safe and sound, none of it was all that bad.

Not as bad as Saint Lucia, I allow myself to think, not for the first time today. Though, my stomach twists at the lie. The trip wasn't awful. Did it end horribly? Yes.

But for those few days when I was with Owen, I was the me I wish I'd always been. I didn't hide a single part of me other than my real feelings. Owen didn't make me feel bad about my choices. He didn't judge my lack of makeup or fancy clothes.

He accepted me when I felt at my worst, and even though I avoided any type of serious conversations with him—because that was what I believed I needed—I thought he was beginning to care about me for more than the crazy, passionate sex we were having.

But if that were true, he never would have been with that woman. He never would have let her touch him like she was or smile down at her like he wanted to eat her for dessert. I never would have had to run away in my pathetic attempt to keep from admitting that I'd let Owen in and he'd disappointed me just like everyone else.

I tilt my head against the car roof, staring up at the twinkling lights above me, and do my best to clear my mind. I don't get to see the stars as openly from home, thanks to all the city lights, but out here, life is freeing. Maybe I could buy an isolated cabin and forget about all my problems that way.

I laugh to myself. Right. A cabin in the woods would be great until I got so bored that I started bringing wild animals into my house and talking to them like people.

It's late and I should go home, but I'm not ready. At least, I'm not until the rain starts. Though, even now, I'm not in a hurry to take cover from the weather. I let the droplets come down on me and wash away the dirt from the day, hoping it will take away a few other things at the same time.

Ten peaceful minutes later, my clothes are soaked through, but my smile has grown even bigger than before.

Only then do I get back in my car and head home.

Today was a good day. Today was exactly what I needed, but I know I'm not done with my soul searching. I want the adrenaline rush I had on the water back in Saint Lucia. I want to feel like I'm flying and free from all my worries, even if it's only for a few seconds.

———

"YOU ARE GOING TO GET YOURSELF KILLED, Ella. I won't allow it," Kenzie says with a glare through our video chat.

"No, I'm not," I reply when I set my phone on the counter so they can still see me while I finish getting ready.

"As much as I hate this idea, I have to agree with Ella. Only 1-in-500,000 people die from bungee jumping, and there have only been five deaths in the last seven years," Piper says.

I grin at my data-obsessed friend. "Thank you, Pipe."

Kenzie talks over me. "Yeah, five people that have been reported. Who knows how many deaths were covered up to prevent lawsuits?"

I shake my head. "Always the lawyer's daughter."

"Damn right, but I'm smarter than all those suits because I didn't become one, much to my father's dismay."

I grab two bottles of water and toss them into my small bag. "You guys are just jealous I didn't invite you."

Kenzie barks out a loud laugh. "Hard pass, bro. Bungee jumping, sky diving, or anything else idiotic that includes some sort of free fall that you might get a hard-on for you won't ever find me doing."

Piper tilts her head. "I might do skydiving. If you become an adrenaline junkie, I expect to at least be invited to the next big thing."

"You got it, but honestly, I was in more danger on the trails yesterday than I will be today on the bridge. I promise."

"Famous last words," Kenzie mutters.

I chuckle. "Always so dramatic."

"Just wait until you see what I put on your headstone if you die today," she retorts.

Piper waves her hand in the screen. "No more talks of death and headstones. Ella is going to do something wild and crazy, but she's doing it for her and that's important. Supporting her asinine choices are what best friends are for." Piper pauses and bites her lip. "Though, as much as I want to stay on the phone until the last minute with you Ella, I need to call my boss. I got an email from the moving company that the truck was canceled. I know it's still supposed to be several months away, but I don't know why they would have canceled."

"Maybe the construction for the building you're waiting on to be finished was shut down. Happens all the time," Kenzie says a little too excitedly. I want to echo that hope, but I know that's not what our friend needs.

"Let us know if something happened. If the date has been moved up, we need to know right away. If it's been pushed back, then hopefully your work has a backup plan for you," I say, trying to be optimistic for Piper.

She's been looking forward to this promotion as editor for weeks. As much as I don't want Piper to leave us, I would never want to hold her back from her dreams.

"I wish I didn't agree with Ella, but please know that I do, Pipe," Kenzie adds.

"I love you both. I'll let you know what I find out. Ella, I expect a video from you as soon as you have it. Don't be a cheap ass and not pay for that footage," Piper says and points at me through the screen.

I nod. "I promise there will be proof provided."

"Talk to you crazy bitches later," Kenzie says and blows us kisses before ending the video chat.

I take a deep breath and head for the garage. It's time for me to leave anyway, because if I wait around any longer, I might just chicken out.

I toss the small bag I packed with waters and granola bars into my front seat before opening the garage door. My fingers grip the keys to start the car when I see Gavin walking into my garage.

"Can we talk, please?" he asks.

Apparently, avoiding my problems until Monday isn't going to be an option.

I get out of my car and close the door so I can lean against it. When I look closer at Gavin, his golden eyes are red with dark circles beneath them. The buttons on his shirt are out of line, and his khaki pants are wrinkled. I almost feel bad he's so out of sorts, but I don't.

"What do you want, Gavin?" I ask when he stands there silently.

"I want to apologize," he replies.

I laugh. "I don't need your apologies. I just need you to leave me alone."

He shoves his hands in his pockets and rocks back and forth on his heels. "Listen, I fucked up, and I know I don't deserve you back, but I just needed you to know I've felt like shit ever since that day. I wasn't seeing that chick and I don't intend to in the future, regardless of what happens between us. I regret ever talking to her."

I let out a small sigh. "While I appreciate the gesture, this doesn't change anything, Gavin. Our relationship is over. I can forgive you and move on, but not with you."

His jaw hardens and he nods. "I figured, but I had to try. You're an incredible woman, Ella. I'm sorry I didn't make you feel that way when I had the opportunity."

His words cut almost as deeply as his betrayal. If he'd spoken to me this way when we were together, I might have cared for him more, but after looking back, I realize we were more like roommates with benefits than we ever were a couple.

"Thank you," I say earnestly.

He stands there, looking at everything other than me. "Maybe I'll see you around."

I watch his retreating form and breathe a sigh of relief. It's done. I have my closure with Gavin and can truly move on. Whatever there was between us, it's officially over. I had wanted to postpone that moment, but only because I was afraid. Now that it's passed, that fear is gone and I feel so much lighter.

I gave Gavin two years of my life, and I was furious when he cheated, but thinking about that night with a clearer mind, I was madder at myself. Mad for letting him stay so long and mad for not knowing when to walk away from the relationship neither of us were overly happy in.

Maybe I'd been wrong in wanting a weekend alone. Maybe I should have spent this time facing my problems so I can start anew all that much sooner. Hell, maybe I'd even been wrong running from what happened in Saint Lucia. Except it's too late to worry about that.

Owen isn't here. He isn't even reaching out anymore. If I was as important as I thought I was to him, I would have heard from him again, regardless of whether I'd been ignoring his prior attempts.

I need to forget about the feelings I was trying to deny for him and remember that there's nothing wrong with being alone and happy with myself. If, or when, I ever cross paths with Owen Porter again, I'll at least know that facing him is better than running.

After I get back in my car, I send off a text to Piper

and Kenzie, summarizing what happened before beginning to back out of the garage. I'm not even out of the driveway before I hear the ping of a response.

Kenzie: I'm so fucking proud of you, Ella. You are a woman to be admired. Go kick ass at bungee jumping...and please don't die. I love you!

I wait a second longer, but when there isn't anything immediate from Piper, I know she's busy with work stuff, which I hope for her is a good thing.

Without anything else to stop me, I reverse the rest of the way and head to the bridge where I hope to let go of the rest of my worries.

Today is going to be a great day. I won't let it be any other way.

Chapter Twenty-Seven

JUMP OFF A BRIDGE

Owen

A DAY AND A HALF HAVE PASSED SINCE I GOT back to Charlotte. I've kept my phone on me at all times in case Ella or her friend reaches out, but I haven't answered any other calls or texts.

Bill sent some updates, but I can't find it within myself to reply. I nearly let my job turn me into the kind of person I never wanted to be. Even if they succeed in firing Jack, without drastic changes within the company, I'm not even sure I want my job back if offered. I don't want to work for another asshole who may not be as bad as Jack, but will undoubtedly only care about one thing: making money regardless of who gets hurt in the process.

Tomorrow, when I know Human Resources is back in the office, I'll formally quit in person. Jack won't be back from Saint Lucia yet, and it will also give me the opportunity to grab my stuff without anyone causing a scene. That thought loosens a small amount of the unease I've been feeling for the last couple of days.

Honoring Kenzie's request and not reaching out to Ella is harder than I thought it would be. My time with Ella was short, but I can't get her out of my mind. Not even when I sleep.

I miss her warmth and her laugh and the way she made me smile for no reason. I barely got to know her, but I'm craving more. If Kenzie hasn't reached out by tomorrow morning, I'll consider going back to my own methods.

As if my mere thoughts conjured her, Kenzie's name flashes on my phone. I answer on the first ring. "Kenzie?"

"Someone's eager," she says.

"Did you expect anything less?" I ask.

"I guess not."

"How's Ella?" I ask when her pause is too long.

"She's doing better than I thought she would be. I realize something for the better happened to her in Saint Lucia and, while she won't admit it, I think you had a little to do with that something."

Damn, I sure hope so.

"So, do you think she'll talk to me?" I ask.

She pauses again, and the silence makes my stomach churn. "I think so, but if she turns you away and you don't respect her choice, me and you are going to have problems. I'm breaking all the best friend rules and I won't be happy if Ella isn't."

I clear my throat, thankful she can't see me grinning. "I would never disrespect Ella. You have my word. Is she at home? Should I call her again?"

"She's not home and probably won't answer her phone right now. If you want to see her today, you're going to have to be prepared to jump off a bridge."

My eyes widen. "Uh, come again?"

Heights are not my thing. I can look out windows and appreciate views, but walking over bridges, going up ladders, things like that? Not a fan.

"Apparently, Saint Lucia turned our girl into an adrenaline junkie. She's going bungee jumping. You can try to join her or meet her at the bottom, but the first would likely impress her more," Kenzie says.

"Right. Of course it would," I reply with a slight groan.

"Well, I've done all I'm willing to do. The rest is up to you and Ella. If you upset her again, I will find you."

I believe her, but I also hope there won't be any reason for her to follow through on the threat. "Thank you, Kenzie."

"You're not welcome. I'm risking a lot by doing this. I just hope my instincts are right about you. I'll text you the address of where to go," she says then hangs up.

I make a mental note to find a way to pay back Kenzie, regardless of how things work out—that's the least she deserves for helping me—then hurry to get my shoes on.

I don't want to miss my chance to find Ella at the top

of that bridge. I need to know if there's any chance she can forgive me. And, if she feels the same as I do about her, I intend to find out even if it means jumping off a bridge.

I might hate heights, but there's no way I'm waiting for Ella at the bottom. She deserves better than that from me...and so much more.

———

An hour later, I'm parked on the side of the road at the spot Kenzie texted me the address for. I can't see Ella, but that doesn't mean she's not here. I take a few deep breaths before getting out of my car. My hands are shaking, and I'm sweating more than should be natural underneath my purposely chosen black polo, but hopefully Ella won't notice how freaked out I am.

With semi-forced steps, I head for where I can see people gathering. There are six men and women gathered around, and I can see a metal platform secured to the bridge with bungee cords hanging from the chain link.

My chest is burning. I don't understand why Ella wants to do this.

A woman turns around. "Oh, are you Brad?"

I shake my head, unable to speak.

"Jumper number two might be a no show," the woman announces to the others.

A man heads to the van behind them. "I'll give him a call."

When he moves out of the way, I catch my first sight of Ella since I left her sleeping in the hotel Thursday morning. Any fear that's been growing inside me is smothered by the awe of how stunning she is to me.

Her hair is braided down her back. She's wearing dark jeans and a white tank top that clings to her sides. I want to reach for her, but I know I don't have that right. Not yet, anyway. I hope "yet" is the right word to use.

She looks down at her side closest to me and tugs on one of the straps around her waist. "Are you sure this—"

Our eyes lock, and she stops talking mid-sentence.

I take a step further, but she shakes her head, stopping me mid-stride. "What are you doing here, Owen?"

"I came to..." I'm not sure how to say what I need to with the other five people present now watching us.

"Came to what?" Ella demands.

I step forward, even though she doesn't seem to want me closer. I don't want to have this conversation feeling like we're yelling at each other.

"I came to apologize and explain what you saw," I finally say when she's only five-or-so feet from me.

Ella scoffs. "Oh, that's not necessary. You and Natalie make a wonderful couple. I hope the two of you are happy together."

"She's not the one I want," I plead with a desperation I'm not at all ashamed of.

The group of workers begin to disperse, and I move until I'm standing in front of Ella. She takes a step back, but she can't go far. She's already strapped into a harness that not only goes around her thighs and waist, but also crosses over her chest. At her feet, thick wraps are secured around her ankles and carabiners secure the bungee to her.

"Ella, I left that morning because Bill wanted to meet with me. He asked me to get closer to Jack, so I could retrieve some information for the board. The only way I could get back in that asshole's good graces was to pretend to like Natalie. She knew it was all a show. She doesn't mean anything to me, and she doesn't have feelings for me. All she wanted was my help."

Ella's eyes are narrowed, and she crosses her arms. "Didn't seem that way when I saw you smiling down at her in the hotel."

"The only happiness I had in that moment was knowing our day was nearly over and that I was another minute closer to finding you," I say, hoping like hell she believes me.

She doesn't say anything, and the lack of distraction has me shaking when I make the mistake of looking to my right. The edge of the bridge is right there. A few more steps and I could fall right to my death.

I realize the chance of that happening is slim-to-none, but my mind isn't accepting logic right now.

"Are you okay?" Ella asks, taking me by surprise with her concern.

I nod. "Just not a fan of heights that could get me killed."

"Right. Well, as long as you're not dying, then I think we're done here," she says, and that little bit of hope I had is dashed away.

"Ella, please give me a chance. I will face any fear for you. I will climb to the tallest mountain. I will jump off this damn bridge if it proves to you that I mean every word I'm saying. I don't want to lose you. I can't."

Her eyes soften, but her stance remains firm. "Why, Owen? Why can't you lose me? You've only just met me."

I take a step forward, my hands itching to touch her, but I won't do so without her permission. "I can't, because I know that any day without you in it won't be as bright. I don't want to go days without hearing your laugh or the clicking of your tongue when you're concentrating. I want to live for the moments that I get to hold you in my arms. I want to be the reason you smile and be the person who wipes away your tears when you're sad, not the one to cause them. I can't lose you, because there is so much I don't want to experience without you by my side."

Ella's lips tremble, and I continue, "I don't want to further upset you, Ella. I only came here to say the truth and beg for your forgiveness, but if you want me to go, I will. I don't want you to hurt anymore because of me. I just had to make sure you knew that Natalie is nothing to me. In fact, I quit my job that same day. As soon as I knew you were gone, I was done with Harrington

Enterprises. Nothing else mattered to me besides finding you."

"Why did you stop calling me, then?" Ella asks, and a few tears fall down her cheeks.

"Because your best friend thought that it would be better if I gave you space. Believe me, I didn't want to, but I also didn't want to hurt you anymore."

Her eyes darken. "Kenzie? Is she how you found me here?"

I nod. "But she told me nothing else. Don't be mad at her. If you're still angry, yell at me."

Ella sighs and rubs her hands over her face. "I'm not angry, Owen. I'm hurt, and I'm scared, and I just want to jump off this bridge."

"Then, let's do that. Let me jump with you," I say, even though I'll probably die from a heart attack before I get to the bottom.

She lowers her hands from her face. "You'd do that even though you're about to piss your pants right now?"

I finally reach for her, gently gripping her hand. "I'd do anything for you, Ella."

She sucks in a breath, and I badly want to kiss her plump pink lips, but instead, I let go of her hand and walk to the van where the employees are trying and failing to hide that they're listening to us.

"So, can I jump with her?" I ask.

A woman with a huge smile and tears brimming in her eyes nods. "This is the sweetest thing ever. Of course, you can jump. The other guy canceled anyway. Too scared of dying."

I cringe. "I didn't really need to know that."

"Right. Sorry."

A guy slaps a hand on my shoulder. "Let's get you strapped in, man."

This is insane, and I never should have told Ella I'd jump, but I couldn't let her do this without me. I need her to know that no matter how afraid I am, I'll always be by her side. I won't be like her exes. I won't cheat. I won't leave. I won't ever let her go.

I just need Ella to give me a second chance.

Chapter Twenty-Eight

DEATH WAS IMMINENT

Ella

Seeing Owen on this bridge is the last thing I expect. I don't know whether I want to yell at him or jump him. The latter surprises me, but I don't show it. Instead, I cross my arms and listen to him spew words I'm trying not to believe.

But the longer he talks and the closer he gets to me, the more I want to believe everything. I don't want Owen to be just like every other guy I dated before him. Except, it doesn't matter how much I want that. I can't change who Owen is, and he showed me who that is both times I saw him with Natalie, along with the amount of shit he put up with from Jack.

At least, that's what I think until Owen confesses that he quit working for that douchebag. That he's walked away from everything he'd already told me he wanted merely because he wanted me more.

He's saying everything I've always wished a man would say, but I don't know if I can trust Owen. The risk is too great. I already know after only spending a few days with him that he's the kind of man I could lose myself to.

I can't ever be that vulnerable again. I can't give him the power to hurt me.

"I'm going to jump with you, Ella," Owen says, making me flinch when he returns from talking to the employees.

"You can't do that," I reply.

He already looks close to passing out. I can't imagine what jumping will do to him. His skin is pale and pasty. His hands and arms are shaking, and there is a layer of sweat shining over his exposed skin.

"I can, Ella. I want you to know that no matter what, I'll always jump with you. You don't have to be afraid. Even if you're not ready for anything serious, as long as you don't send me away, I'm going to be right here, in whatever capacity you'll have me."

Mother shit. It's like he can read my mind. It's been that way since the first day at the hotel. He knew what I needed with Blake. He knew what I needed in his room. He's known when to push and when not to this entire time.

All of those things I refused to see or accept when we'd been on the island, but being back at home, seeing him here now, I can't deny that, somehow, in just a matter of days, Owen Porter has figured me out.

"Unless you'd rather do this on your own," Owen adds when I don't respond to his prolific words.

"No. I mean, only if you really want to. I'm not here to tell you what to do," I reply, but I've lost the conviction in my voice from earlier.

"Ella, your wants and needs are just as important as anyone else's. If jumping from this bridge on your own is what you need, then I'll meet you at the bottom. If you just want me gone, then I'll do that, too, regardless of how much it pains me to walk away from you. None of what I said means anything unless you believe me and want me here."

Damn him for making me feel. Damn him for coming here and showing me the truth. Damn him for facing his fears and making me feel strong enough to do the same.

"I don't want you to go, Owen. I don't know what that means after we get to the bottom, but I know that having you at my side when I jump isn't the worst thing that could happen today. I know that I've missed you even when I didn't want to, that I've thought of you even when I tried otherwise. Craved you when I shouldn't have, but I can't promise I'm ready for anything more than what we had on the island. I need time."

He steps forward and cups my cheeks with the biggest grin on his face. "Ella Danes, all you have to do is ask and I'll give you whatever you want. Even if it's time."

I reach for his shirt and pull him closer. I need to feel his lips on mine and to taste him on my tongue before we jump. Waiting another minute longer isn't possible after all our revelations.

Owen's hands burrow into my braided hair, and I keep a tight hold on his shirt. Our tongues battle for dominance as if no time has passed since I last kissed him.

It's only when one of the employees clears their throat that Owen pulls back. "I guess it's time to strap up."

His voice is sure, but he's still shaking.

"You don't have to do this," I say.

He steps into the first of many straps that he'll be hooked to. "Yes, I do. For many reasons. If I'm going to ask you to let go of your fears and trust me, then I need to do the same."

"Okay," I reply with a wink.

His eyes narrow at me and his lip curls, but he can't get any closer to me while being secured to the bungee.

Letting Owen jump from the bridge with me and not telling him to leave isn't what I thought would happen if I ever saw him again, but there is nothing about having him next to me that feels wrong. I wasn't sure I could ever trust another man again, especially not one I've only just met, but I don't want to ignore my gut or my heart. Both of which say Owen is worth keeping around.

"Alright, we'll do one more check on both of your

harnesses, and then we're good to go," the woman who previously strapped me in says.

She grins widely at me when I nod, and I'm surprised I don't feel at all embarrassed that possibly one of the most impactful moments of my life unfolded in front of a handful of strangers.

Another guy pulls on the buckles around my chest, waist, and ankles before guiding me forward on the deck we'll be jumping from. Owen is ghost white while he shuffles his way toward me.

While they're securing helmets to both of us, I reach my hand out, and he puts his trembling fingers in my grasp. "You'll feel much better when we get to the bottom," I say.

"Ha, it will be a miracle if I can feel anything at all by then."

One of the male crew members steps right behind us on the platform. "Alright, you two. I need you to relax and bend your knees. When you're ready, you can jump. Your freefall will only last a few seconds and then you'll be jerked back up. Don't worry about screaming, everyone does. Even the men. You'll swing and bounce around until we lower you onto the airbag waiting for you at the bottom. That's normal. The cameras on your heads are on, so let's have some fun!"

I keep hold of Owen's hand and give it a squeeze. "Are you ready?"

"Absolutely not, but if you count, I'll follow your

lead," he says without looking at me. His gaze seems to be locked on the treetops in front of us.

Owen's fears and the desire to be strong for him have pushed any of my own worries aside. It's something I'm rather thankful for. I don't want to postpone the jump any longer, so I begin counting.

"One...two...three!" I shout and push off the platform.

Owen's grip stays with mine for a split second until we're free falling. My stomach is in my chest, blood is rushing to my head, and I'm screaming so loudly I probably won't have a voice when I'm back on two feet, but the euphoric feeling is worth every formidable second while we head face first toward the ground.

My arms flail, and my screams turn into shouts of joy. Owen on the other hand is flailing his arms so hard that I'm afraid he's going to break something. When we bounce back up for the first time, his body goes limp and I call his name several times.

There's no response and I start to get worried that I actually did kill him.

"Owen!" I shout louder than before when I'm able to catch more of my breath.

He finally groans and his eyes roll around. Oh, thank fuck he's not dead.

The jerking motions from the bungee are minor, and I give Owen a moment to fully find his awareness again.

When he lifts his hands to his face, I ask, "Are you going to survive over there?"

He grunts in reply, but he's moving more. I take that as a good sign, even if he can't find his voice yet.

I try to hide the smile on my face that's partly in thanks to his obvious torture. I might have forgiven him enough to let him jump with me, but seeing him go through a bit of torment isn't a hardship whatsoever. Even if he hadn't meant to, Owen put me through hell, and this combined with the apology he already gave is the perfect beginning to us starting over.

A few minutes later, when we're laying on our backs on the ginormous airbag, I glance over at Owen and he's finally smiling.

"What has you so happy?" I ask.

"I didn't die. I was absolutely certain death was imminent."

"Such a drama queen," I tease.

His face turns serious. "I missed you, Ella. So damn much."

Owen's hand is open and waiting for me to accept it. My first thought is to do so, and I listen. "I missed you, too."

For the first time in much too long, I'm not afraid, and that's the best feeling in the world.

Chapter Twenty-Nine

LUCKY BASTARD

Owen

IT'S BEEN THREE WEEKS SINCE WE CAME BACK from Saint Lucia, and it's been the best of my life. Ella has kept me at arm's length, as expected, but the benefits have been worth every day I wait for her to feel ready for another serious relationship. Even if it takes months for that to happen, I'll still be right here waiting.

I've been properly courting her ever since I jumped off that damn bridge and almost died. Weekly dates, outings with her friends because I know how special they are to her, flowers, and breakfast in bed on those couple of nights I've gotten lucky enough to stay the night with her.

Today is extra special, though. Today is her thirtieth birthday, and I plan to woo the hell out of her in hopes she'll finally allow me to at least call her my girlfriend.

Kenzie and Piper stayed with her last night. Apparently, it's a birthday tradition to have sleepovers on the night before so that they can be the first to wish a happy birthday to whoever is the honorary bestie—their words, not mine.

I'm only mildly jealous, but when I think about what I have planned for tonight, I know I have no reason to be. Reservations to her favorite restaurant have been secured, I have a black pearl necklace wrapped in my glove box, and after dinner, she'll get her favorite dessert: my dick.

Only when I've turned her into mush do I plan to pop the girlfriend question. Devious? Yes. Meant to be a sweet gesture? Absolutely.

Me: Happy birthday, beautiful. I'm outside your house with pastries and mimosas

She reads the messages immediately.

Ella: Why isn't your sexy ass inside then?

My grin grows at her response, and I get out of the car with my offerings. I wasn't allowed to crash their sleepover, but nobody objected to the morning after.

Using the code to the door I was given, I let myself in and head to the kitchen, even though I'm dying to go straight to Ella's room. The only thing keeping me away is seeing Kenzie or Piper wearing less clothes than I'm comfortable with.

I hear footfalls coming from the hallway and hurry to make the first mimosa. I hold the glass out just in time to see Piper appear instead of Ella.

"Well, don't you look disappointed. That's

adorable," she says with a wink before stealing the glass from my hand and heading to sit at the counter.

I sigh and make another, hoping the next face I see is Ella's.

Another minute later, I've prepared two more mimosas while Piper debates out loud to herself over whether she should take the chocolate or glazed pastry.

Kenzie shows up next, and I roll my eyes at her devious smirk. She waltzes over to me and kisses my cheek before stealing both glasses from me. "Good morning, Owen. Don't you feel so lucky to be serving the three most beautiful ladies in North Carolina on this fine day?"

"Oh, so lucky," I deadpan.

Ella finally appears and my hands are empty. Instead of reaching for the champagne, I take two steps forward and scoop her into my arms, dipping her backward before whispering, "Happy birthday, Ms. Danes."

"Why thank you, Mr. Porter," she says with a light squeal before I press my lips to hers.

Her hands grip my hair, and she opens to me. I wasn't going to devour her in front of her friends, but if this is what she wants first thing on her birthday, then that's what my woman is going to get.

Something soft yet heavy hits the back of my head. "Get a room!" Kenzie yells.

Ella's right hand releases my hair, and I assume she's flipping her best friend off. "Go home if you can't handle the heat," Ella says when I bring her back up.

"Ha! Good luck getting rid of me," Kenzie replies.

Piper elbows her. "You have work to do today."

"Yeah, adulting at its finest," Kenzie grumbles.

I follow Ella to the counter and say, "Speaking of work, that's my first surprise. I took today off so we can go shopping, to the spa, hiking, or whatever you want to do."

Her vibrant green eyes widen with a spark of joy. "Seriously?"

"As soon as you told me you weren't working, I knew I couldn't leave you here alone."

Piper scoffs. "Um, hello? I would have happily stayed with her."

"Don't you have books to read for work?" Ella asks pointedly.

"Maybe." Piper grins. She's started her new position as editor, but most of her job is virtual until the building she'll be working in gets finalized. Unfortunately for Piper, she has no idea when that's going to be, thanks to some permits not getting filed on time.

"So, does that sound like a way to spend your special day followed by dinner at Antonio's?" I ask Ella when I finish making her a drink.

She nudges me with her hip and steals the glass from my hand. "Duh. I'll get ready and we'll head out to the trails for the morning and figure out the rest later."

Ella has been outside, doing anything to get her heart rate pulsing every chance she's had since we've been back, so it's no surprise to hear that's what she wants to do today instead of shopping or being pampered.

I lean in to give Ella another kiss, because I can't get enough of her. "I just need to send an email to the board while you get ready."

Kenzie is out of her seat, getting a pastry when she elbows me in the ribs. "You know, if there are any eligible bachelors at your work that aren't d-bags like your old boss, I'm single and ready to mingle."

I laugh. "Oh, Kenzie. I don't think any of them could handle you."

She grins. "Probably not, but just in case there's one, don't forget about your woman's single and hot friends."

"I'll see what I can do," I say, even though there's not a chance in hell that I'd ever play matchmaker with Ella's friends. That's the kind of potential drama I don't want in my life.

Though, ever since the board was able to get the information that they needed to fire Jack, things have been better. Apparently, they hadn't needed me after all. Not when one of the IT guys was able to hack into Jack's laptop and get the needed information.

Once that was all finalized, the board offered me the role of Marketing Vice President, and things have been a lot calmer in my work life. I didn't think I would go back to what is now only called West-to-East, Inc., but Bill was relentless with his calls and offers.

So far, he and the other board members have followed through on every single promise they made to me, including getting rid of all the employees who favored the type of dealings that Jack preferred and hiring a new younger CEO who spends some of his summers volunteering in third world countries instead of harassing women. I hope he proves to be worth the wait for the growing company once he officially starts.

Ella finishes her drink and sets it on the counter before leaving the kitchen. "I'll be back as quick as I can be."

I smack her ass when her back is to me. "Don't be long or I'll have to come find you."

She half-turns around and winks. "See you soon, then."

Kenzie pretends to gag, and Piper is shaking her head when I glance at them. I thought Ella having such close friends would be an annoyance, but so far, they've only been supportive of me and my drive to make Ella happy.

Though, I won't be sad when they find their own men—without my help—to keep them occupied a little more often, because having them here and in no hurry to leave when I really want to go give Ella a birthday fucking in the shower isn't what I call fun.

Instead of feeling put out, I tell myself that I could be holed up in my office, alone and unhappy. That thought is enough of a reminder to have me smiling and more than grateful to be here in Ella's house, being the lucky bastard who gets to take care of her on her special day.

And hopefully for many more days, weeks, months, and years to come.

Epilogue

THE HAPPY ENDING

Ella

OUR WILD SUMMER IS ALMOST OVER, AND normally, I'm not one to want an end to the warmer weather, but when I think about weekends with Owen, locked away thanks to snow and rain... Well, winter doesn't sound so bad.

I've spent the last three months letting him in further by the day. When he asked me to be his girlfriend on my birthday, it was the sweetest gesture. I'd known then that there was no way I was going to let him go, but I'd still needed to do things on my own terms.

Which is how we've ended up alone, on the coast in Myrtle Grove, for the weekend. I told him we needed to celebrate our small relationship milestone, and while he went out and planned a fancy dinner, took me shopping down in the main parts of town to the boutiques, I have been concocting another agenda for the rest of our evening.

Owen has told me he loves me so many times that I've lost count. The first time, the words had accidentally spilled from his lips, and he apologized profusely, but I reassured him that there was nothing wrong with telling me how he feels, as long as he wasn't offended that I didn't say the words back. At least, not yet.

Thankfully, he wasn't, and since then, I've shown him how I feel in my own ways, on my own time. Like tonight, I'm wearing his favorite silk dress that he bought me in Saint Lucia for the welcome mixer, and the pearls he gave me on my birthday are hanging from my neck.

But it's the small touches that I hope convey the most meaning to Owen. When I brush the back of my hand against his, when I lean my head against his shoulder, or when we embrace and there is never a time when I'm ready to let go.

Owen smiles down at me when we walk back into the rented house after our dinner on the pier. His white button-up shirt is tucked into grey slacks, and the green tie he said he wore because it matched my eyes hangs loosely around his neck.

I grab on to the tie and yank him toward the bedroom. "I'm rather tired from our eventful day," I purr.

He raises a brow. "Is that so?" Then, he hurries forward to scoop me into his arms. "I guess I better get you to bed then."

I bat my eyes at him, then feign a yawn. "I guess so."

We enter the master bedroom, and he settles me onto the mattress. I move back and sprawl out, letting my arms relax above my head while my feet still dangle off the edge.

When I look back up at Owen, his eyes are dark, and he's licking his lips while he slowly unbuttons his shirt.

"If you keep staring at me like that, I'll never get any sleep, Mr. Porter," I tease and spread my legs a little farther apart.

He knows what I want. He always has.

Owen steps closer, tossing his shirt onto the ground once he gets to the foot of the bed.

Need courses through me, and my heart races. What I have planned isn't conventional by anyone's standards, but this is what feels right to me, and I don't intend to back down from my plan.

I prop myself up on my elbows, and my face heats as I watch him intently remove his pants and shoes. When he's down to only black boxer briefs, Owen grabs the backs of my knees and pulls me until my ass is teetering on the edge of the mattress.

"How about we end the best day ever with the best orgasm ever?" he suggests with a waggle of his brows.

"Oh, how you spoil me," I say faintly.

His lips turn up, offering me my favorite smile. "And what a pleasure it is for me to do so."

Owen's hands move over my thighs until his fingers capture the ends of my dress. He tugs the material up and over my head, then tosses the fabric onto the chair in the corner of the room.

He stares into my eyes, stroking my cheek with one hand while he undoes my bra with the other. His lips move as if he wants to say something, but he holds back, and I smile before leaning up to capture his lips.

My tongue devours his mouth, and he finishes getting us undressed while managing to never break our kiss. His dick twitches against my pussy, and I lean back, wrapping my legs around his hips, urging him closer.

His fingers follow the line of my slit, and he hums. "Always so eager."

"Only for you."

Before I get the three words out, his cock slams inside me and my back arches, moans already growing inside me.

His movements slow into long steady strokes that have me needy and begging. "Owen, please."

He reaches down and wraps his arms around me until he can lift me up enough to move us further back onto the bed. I watch his blue eyes darken as he gets us resituated and enjoy the throbbing of his dick inside me.

My hips lift, needing more from him and he delivers beyond my expectations.

He brushes strands of my hair out of my face and cups my cheek before kissing me softly. I want to tell him how I feel so badly, but I wait for the perfect moment.

His kisses turn sweet. No battle of tongues, just

sensual caresses that have my insides tightening, and I know I can't wait much longer.

I push on his chest until Owen begins to roll over and I'm on top. I want him to watch my face, to know that everything I've grown to love about myself and life and everything in between is because he had the patience to let me do things my way and the faith to know that one day, I would be ready for more.

As I lean forward, getting the angle right where I love him most, I'm reminded again how thankful I am that we finally ditched the condoms once both of us were tested and I re-upped my birth control. No babies for us, but maybe one day.

Owen's hips move in time with the roll of my own, and my eyes close while I let my mouth fall open. My hand is pressed against his chest, using it for leverage while I grind against him, finding the pleasure I know only he can give me.

His hands move down and grip my ass, pushing me forward and somehow going deeper inside me. I gasp and cry out, and I'm nearly there. Owen must know it, too, because his hold tightens, keeping me in place while breathing becomes harder and harder to do.

My moans grow louder, and the walls of my pussy squeeze around his magnificent cock. I expect him to slow his movements, but instead, he shifts his position and drives harder inside me.

"Right there. Do not stop," I pant, barely able to get the words out.

He thrusts faster and deeper and holds on to my ribs while I bounce above him. His stomach muscles ripple from the added effort, and my fingers trace over the sculpted lines until I throw my head back, right on the edge of release.

Owen sits up and grabs the back of my neck and lower back, changing our angle again. I hold on to his shoulders, riding him hard until my body tenses and I see stars in my eyes. My skin tingles, and I shudder as his grip attempts to keep me from falling completely apart in his arms.

He continues to rock gently beneath me, telling me he didn't finish while I exploded around him, but he's there waiting for me, just like always, when I come back down from the high he delivered so expertly.

Once clarity comes back to me, I lift my hands and cup his cheeks. I press my lips to his and smile softly at the joy I see in his eyes that only see me. I know immediately that this is my time. The perfect time.

"I love you, Owen Porter," I say, voice confident and never letting my eyes stray from his.

He stiffens beneath me, and a sheen spreads over his stare. "And I love you. So damn much."

Owen leans in to kiss me over and over, but I'm not done with my surprises and pull back.

"That's good, because there's something I want to ask you," I say, and want to kick myself when I hear trepidation leak through my tone. It's not him I doubt, and I don't want him to think that, but it's harder to control the nerves than I thought it would be.

He sucks in a short breath and stills. "You can ask me anything, Ella."

I bite my lip and feel my cheeks flush. The few moments it takes me to find the right words—that I should know by heart because I've thought of this moment for weeks now—nearly kill me from anticipation.

Owen strokes my cheeks, saying nothing. Once again, he's as patient and kind as I've grown to know and that is all it takes for me to just say what I need to instead of the speech I'd prepared.

"Will you marry me?"

His mouth pops open ever so slightly, his eyes widen, and then he grins. The biggest grin that I've ever seen.

Owen wraps his arms around me, squeezing me until I can barely breathe, then he pulls back enough that he can see my face.

"I will do anything with you, Ella Danes. I will follow you to the ends of Earth. Hell, I'll jump off another bridge with you, but most importantly, I will love you until my dying breath. I will be whatever it is that you need for the rest of our lives, because I'm never going to let you go."

Tears fill my eyes, and my own smile grows as I laugh softly. "You could have just said yes."

He shakes his head. "Not when you surprise the hell out of me like that."

I press my forehead to his, and my sigh is full of happiness. "I don't want to wait for anything with you, Owen. You've shown me what true happiness is. Your patience is a gift that I won't ever take advantage of and deserves to be rewarded. I want to be yours in every way possible for as long as possible."

He sucks in a breath, and I'm probably going to have bruises from all his strong embraces, but each one will be absolutely worth it. There's nothing grander in this world than knowing this man loves me with his whole heart.

His lips press quickly to mine, and his hips swivel, reminding me that he's still buried deep inside me. "I'm going to make love to you all night long, Ella Danes-soon-to-be-Porter."

Owen reverses our roles, and I let out giggles of unfiltered happiness. "That is something that I'll never turn down."

"Not even when we're old and wrinkly?" he teases, stroking my cheek with the back of his fingers.

"Not even then." I press a gentle kiss onto his hand, blinking once and staring into his eyes, sharing the words I couldn't get out earlier.

"Thank you, Owen. Thank you for always knowing what I need. For loving me without words. For allowing me the time I needed without making me feel selfish. For being so perfectly you. And for believing in me, even on the days when I didn't believe in myself."

His touch trails lightly over my arm, and he leans

closer until our lips are nearly touching. "No thanks needed, my love. You're mine now, and I'll gladly spend the rest of our lives reminding you of that and so much more."

"Always yours. Now and forever."

———

Thank you for reading *A Mutually Beneficial Proposal*! Do you want a bit more from Ella and Owen? How about a sexy bonus scene? Subscribe to my newsletter HERE to get access today!

Plus, keep flipping the pages to read the first two chapters of Kenzie's story A Mutually Beneficial Mistake which is now available on Amazon and Kindle Unlimited!

Connect with Me

Want to come hang out with me on social media and with other readers who also enjoyed books this one? Join Harper Reed's RomCom Insiders for fun and shenanigans!
Also, check out the many ways to connect with me below!
These are the best ways to stay updated on new releases and sales.

Newsletter—Reader Group—Facebook Page—Instagram—TikTok—Website—Amazon—Bookbub

I look forward to seeing you around!

About the Author

Harper Reed is a Romantic Comedy author. She lives in the beautiful state of Oregon with her husband of twenty years. While Harper is new to the genre, she has been reading RomCom's for decades and has published several dozen books in varying genres over the years.

You can find her other works under Heather Renee.

In her downtime, Harper enjoys reading, going on escapades with her husband, and spending time outdoors.

She looks forward to this new branch of her author career and can't wait to bring you more deliciously comical books!

Want to learn more? Visit her website www.HarperReedBooks.com to see upcoming books and ways to connect with her.

Also by Harper Reed

THE UNEXPECTED SERIES

A Spicy RomCom Trilogy featuring three best friends and their happily-ever-afters!

A Mutually Beneficial Proposal

A Mutually Beneficial Mistake

A Mutually Beneficial Secret

COMING SOON STANDALONES

A Royal Oops

A Spicy RomCom with royal antics, an oops marriage, and a kingdom that needs their new queen.

Releasing early 2023!

Date Bait

A Spicy RomCom about woman who has tried and failed to get the attention of her brother's sexy best friend. Now, it's time to up the ante.

Releasing in 2023!

The Fire Next Door

A Spicy RomCom about single dad fireman and his new, attractive neighbor that soon finds herself bringing by more than chocolate chip cookies.

Releasing late 2023!

Now Available!

A Mutually Beneficial Proposal is the first book in The Unexpected Series consisting of three interconnected standalones, all ending with a happily-ever-after for the two main characters. Each story will be filled with laugh-out-loud scenes, spice, and growth by your favorite characters.

Read *A Mutually Beneficial Mistake* today with Amazon and Kindle Unlimited. Then, the final book *A Mutually Beneficial Secret* which is also available now!

Flip the page for a sneak peek of book two!

Preview

Chapter One

dirty little bitches

Kenzie

Eating a banana should *not* turn me on. Except, it's been months since I've been on a date with a man worthy of taking home, and my battery-operated boyfriends can only do so much and for so long. So, here I am, at my desk, surrounded by mostly nerdy computer dudes and feeling needy as fuck with no prospects in sight.

"McKenzie?" a soft but sure voice calls from around my cubical wall.

I turn my head, mentally shaking away my inappropriate thoughts, and find my boss's assistant

Clara standing there in her blue plaid skirt, matching blazer, and black Mary Jane shoes.

"How can I help you?" I ask, trying to keep the trepidation out of my voice. I don't like it when Joslin wants to see me or needs something from me. She's harder on me than on the rest of my co-workers for reasons she's never outright said, but I have my assumptions.

"Mrs. Croft would like to speak with you," Clara says with a smile, but it doesn't quite reach her eyes, making my nerves worse.

I give her a terse nod. "I'll be there just as soon as this program loads that I'm working on."

Clara bites the inside of her cheek and shakes her head. "Mrs. Croft insisted you come right away."

A heavy sigh exits from between my lips. "Of course."

I glance over at Glen who is nearest to me. "Will you make sure this finishes?" Then, I point to my computer.

He pushes his glasses further up his nose and rubs a hand over his shaved, balding head while looking at my screen. "Is that the new project we just launched last week? Shouldn't you already have access to that?"

Sometimes I wonder how some of these guys still have a job. "No, it's the updates we'll be doing in two weeks. I'm testing them today and need this beta version to download first. Just keep an eye on it and don't touch anything unless the computer starts making noises it shouldn't."

His eyes never leave my screen. "Sure thing, Mac."

I grit my teeth. I hate when they call me that, and every employee within our little cubical city knows it. Kenzie is the only shortened version of my name that I prefer, but I don't bother to remind Glen of that. At least not now when Joslin is waiting on me.

Getting up, I see that the assistant is gone, and I make my way toward the boss's office on my own. I never thought I'd find myself working in tech, but after taking a coding class in college just for fun, I found myself enthralled with the problem-solving aspects. It was like taking a Rubik's cube of letters and numbers and finding a way for them to form something useful.

Yes, I realize that sounds incredibly nerdy and boring, but it's a high for me unlike anything else. Well, other than orgasmic sex.

And there I go again, thinking about getting laid when that's the last thing I need to have going through my brain while at work. There isn't a single soul in Global Tech's building that I would date. I don't need that kind of drama in my life. Especially not when most men can't handle a woman who speaks whatever is on her mind.

I like to blame Ella for my recent rise in standards. My best friend had to go and land herself the perfect man that she just got engaged to a couple weeks ago. Now, more often than not, I find my dates boring or inappropriate in all the worst ways.

I give my head a solid shake when I arrive at Joslin's

corner of the fourth floor. Clara quickly smiles at me before going back to shuffling papers on her desk.

My knuckles rap on the door and it pops open. "Mrs. Croft?"

"Come in, McKenzie." Her tone is flat, and when I enter, she's typing furiously on her computer with a glower on her oval face.

Her blonde hair is twisted up into a perfect bun, and she's wearing a sleek gray pantsuit with a crisp white blouse beneath the jacket. Her back is ramrod straight as she types without looking at the keyboard, and I'm in awe with how in control she seems even when she looks pissed.

Oh, shit. Did I screw something up? Did I forget to update a program for one of her projects? If I'm about to get fired, I'm going to... I don't know, but something, because I've been working my ass off these last few months for Global Tech.

"Sit, McKenzie," she says while still typing and without looking at me.

I do as she commands, keeping my ankles crossed as I tug at my green sweater, then wipe my palms over my whitewash jeans. I don't dress up for work. I don't "people" much around here, and there isn't a fancy dress code for my position, so I don't see the point, but I'm suddenly feeling out of place and underdressed sitting at Joslin's desk.

Another minute passes as I switch between twisting

my fingers together and crossing and uncrossing my ankles.

Joslin finally gives me her full attention, her honey eyes peering at me while her thin lips create a flat line. She makes an odd humming noise and then slides a piece of paper across the glass desktop toward me.

Her finger taps on the list of projects that are typed out. "You've worked on all of these, yes?"

I nod, staying quiet because it seems like the safe thing to do until I know why she's called me in here.

"And while you haven't been the lead on all of them, you've overseen their executions, repairs, and updates, right?"

Oh, God. Am I going to get in trouble for doing my job *too* well? Fuck my life.

"Yes, but I didn't mean to overstep. I always asked the lead before I did anything," I say a little too quickly.

Joslin finally grins. "I know, McKenzie. You're not in trouble, so don't have a heart attack. That's paperwork I don't have time to fill out."

I wait for her to laugh at the joke, but the sound never comes.

"So, why am I here?" I finally ask, leaning a little closer to the desk.

Joslin folds her hands in front of her and frowns. "Global Tech is doing some restructuring." She pauses when her computer dings.

She takes her sweet time reading whatever just

popped up on her screen, and I'm nearly dying in my seat while I wait for her to finish that damn sentence.

Her eyes land on me again. "My apologies. It hasn't been a great day for everyone around here, but hopefully, it's about to be for you."

My face scrunches. "What do you mean?"

Joslin leans back in her chair, relaxing for the first time since I walked into her office.

"I've been charged with cutting the dead weight around here and finding proper replacements. As much as it pains me to do this, because I don't want to lose you from the ground level—"

She cuts off again, and her attention is back on her computer.

I want to grab this woman by her suit coat and shake her. She said I wasn't in trouble, but it sure as hell sounds like I'm getting canned.

If that happens...Global Tech is about to see a whole different side of McKenzie Chase.

She begins to mutter. "Stupid, stubborn men. I swear, sometimes I hate my job." Then, she looks at me again and forces a smile to her face. "Again, I apologize for the interruptions."

Damn, Joslin is being too...considerate? Professional? I don't know what, but it's damn sure not her normal. I'm totally getting fired for some stupid bullshit.

"As I was saying, I'm not looking forward to replacing you, but when Frank came to me with this proposal, I knew you were the right person for the job."

I raise a brow and let out a breath. "So, you're not letting me go, but I do have to transfer departments?"

I wasn't sure this was better.

Joslin pulls another paper from her desk and hands it to me. "Yes and no. You're getting a promotion, and while you won't work in the weeds of coding any longer, you'll still be working under me, right here on the fourth floor."

As I accept the paper, I try to focus on the words while she keeps talking.

"The work you've been doing this year hasn't gone unnoticed, McKenzie. Not by me or any of the other managers in our department. You're a lot like I was when I was in your position, and I've only pushed you so hard because I can see what you're capable of. Look this over and tell me what you think."

I hold the sheet between my fingers and scan the contents. A promotion is the last thing I expected or have even thought about, especially one that has me supervising other employees. This one also comes with a pay raise and plenty of other bullet points lined out. Mentions of my own office—no more cubical city— quarterly bonuses, and project management duties capture my eye, and... What's that?

"What does 'volunteer hours' mean exactly?" I ask, looking up at Joslin.

She peeks at the paper where I'm pointing. "Oh, that. All employees in supervisor positions are encouraged to volunteer somewhere locally at least twenty hours a year.

You can use work hours to get them done as long as you're not behind on any projects."

Volunteer? More like volun-*told*.

"If you're unsure where to spend your time, I probably have something for you," she adds when I merely continue to stare at the sheet, not missing the number of zeroes in my new salary.

I wasn't prepared for this kind of offer, but the more I read over the information, the more I'm smiling and nodding.

This could change everything. I've always wanted to work hard for my money and livelihood, and while I've been content with my simple lifestyle, there are certain things I'd love to do. Like buy a house, or go on vacation without having to put half of the trip on a credit card, or buy that stupidly expensive purse I don't actually need, but really want.

"I'll do it," I say.

She grins. "Good. I already told them you'd start as soon as the announcement is made."

I laugh, but before I can say anything, Joslin continues, "I'll email you the information for the volunteer position I think you'd be a good fit for later today or tomorrow. I just need to double check a few things. It may be temporary, but it will fill your quota for this year."

My mouth pops open. "I still have to get twenty hours by the end of the year even though it's already August?"

"If you want a good annual review, then you do." Her computer dings again, and instead of keeping her from other work, I offer my sincere thanks and stand.

She nods and mutters more to herself while I see myself out.

I'm grinning from ear to ear when I exit, and Clara smiles at me, handing me more papers. "Congratulations, McKenzie. Sorry I was quiet before. I didn't want to give anything away."

I chuckle. "I thought I was getting fired, so you did a great job hiding the truth."

She gestures to the papers. "Those are the rest of the information you'll need about your new role in Project Management. Please email me if you have any questions."

"Will do."

There's a skip in my step as I make my way back to my computer, and my mood rises when I find that the program I needed downloaded just as I wanted.

Glen tries to talk to me, but I put my earbuds in. Nobody can ruin this day. I'm going to get my work done, review the papers Clara gave me, and then celebrate with my two best friends Ella and Piper tonight.

***

Those dirty little bitches. They stood me up. I'm sitting at our favorite bar with a margarita pitcher in front of me and three glasses, yet there is only one of me.

Ella's earlier headache turned into a full-blown migraine that has her sleeping next to the toilet, and

Piper had to work late. Sure, she just got a promotion herself, so I can understand, but I don't want to.

I want to laugh and scream and be excited with my girls. Instead, I fill all three glasses on the tabletop and intend to drink each of them myself.

I can at least get drunk before I call for a ride back home. To my studio apartment. With nobody in it. All by myself.

Fuck. I'm supposed to be happy right now. Not moping.

My eyes scan the bar, and I look for anyone else by themselves. Maybe I can invite them to join me. Potential one-night stand or friendly face, it doesn't make a difference. I just don't want to be alone.

The room is surrounded by dark wood beams and cream walls with pipe accents followed by twinkle style lights strung all around, making it rather dim in the bar. A perfect setting when you're drinking and want some privacy, but not so great when you're looking for a new companion.

I sit a little straighter when I spot a young woman carrying a single drink away from the bar. She scans the crowd, passing over me, and her eyes land on the group three tables over. Damn it.

Then, I spot a sexy man in a suit coming in the door. His eyes are icy blue and the first thing I notice. The next is the scowl creasing his face and taking away from his straight jawline and five o'clock shadow.

He adjusts his forest-green tie and glances around.

Our eyes never connect, but I watch him intently. The suit is a perfect fit. Not a seam out of place or a sleeve too short on his well-over-six-foot frame.

My tongue darts out to wet my lips, and I take a long pull of my margarita. Damn. Normally, I'm not attracted to rich, stuffy men and he seems to fit that bill pretty accurately as he takes a seat at the bar—alone—but for him? And tonight? I'm willing to make an exception.

I finish my drink and move to slide out of my metal bar stool, but he pulls a phone from his inner front pocket and starts talking.

Sigh. Maybe I can steal his attention later.

I'm halfway through my second drink and nearly ready to give up on the night when an elderly woman walks into the bar, gasping loudly when the bell over the door rings. Her hand presses against her chest and she glances up at the ceiling before continuing forward.

I chuckle, and our stares meet. I assume she's here to meet someone, but instead, she comes right over to me.

"Where are your friends?" She points a wrinkly finger to the other two glasses.

"At home, being party poopers," I say with a sigh.

Her hands pull up on her light-pink pants. "They should try Depends. Might help them get out more."

She takes a seat, and I offer her the remaining full glass. I watch her sniff the sugared edge, shrug, then take a drink. A small bit dribbles down her lip and lands on her flower print shirt.

"Shit. I just bought this."

I nearly choke at her choice in words. "Put a little rubbing alcohol on it when you're home and it will be just fine after washing."

She looks me up and down with a smirk on her wrinkly face. "Spill a few drinks in your nights?"

I shrug. "Possibly."

"I'm Louise." She extends her hand, and I accept the gesture.

"Kenzie," I say, then finish my second drink and reach for the pitcher to fill it back up.

I didn't intend to party it up with Grandma, but the lonely can't be choosy. I'll take her. Though, my eyes cut to the businessman at the bar again. He would have been an excellent candidate as well.

Louise must follow my stare, because she says, "If you take a picture, you can think of him when you're home later taking care of business."

Once again, I can't breathe, and I end up snorting so loud that half the bar turns our way. Including the hottie from the bar.

He cuts a glare at me while he continues to speak into the phone. Okay, maybe he wouldn't have been a great choice in...whatever my dirty mind was conjuring.

My attention swivels back to Louise. "What brings you out tonight?"

She hiccups, her drink almost half gone already. "This place used to be a speakeasy when I was your age. It's where I met my husband. Today should be our fifty-fifth anniversary, but my Marty passed away last year. I thought revisiting where we met might cheer me up."

My mood turns, and my heart aches for her. I move to reach for her hand on the table and offer my condolences, but she pulls it away.

"I lived most of my life with the most wonderful man in the world and made decades of memories with him and our family. I don't need anyone to be sad for me. If anything, you should be jealous." She smiles and continues sipping her stolen drink.

I laugh, this time quieter. "You know, a few months ago, I would have told you I wasn't in the slightest, but now? Yeah, I think I am."

She nods toward the businessman. "Why don't you go make another new friend and take care of your problem, then?"

I shake my head. "Things aren't as simple as they used to be."

She raises a gray brow at me. "Aren't they, though? You find the person you're attracted to, chat with them, make sure they're not a murderer, and then voila!"

Louise flicks her fingers like she's making fireworks with her hands, and I chuckle again. "You make it sound so easy."

"And your generation makes everything so complicated."

I raise my glass toward her. "Amen, Louise."

We sit in companionable silence while we both enjoy

our margaritas and the classic rock playing from the speakers around the bar.

When Louise finishes first, she sighs and leans forward. "Well, Kenzie, it was lovely to meet you, but I've done what I came here to do. Maybe I'll see you around."

I'm mid-sip when she slips off her stool, and by the time I can use my voice again, she's already halfway to the door.

Loneliness creeps back in, and I find myself looking toward my right for the umpteenth time. Though, I swear to myself that it's not to peek at the hottie's broad shoulders or to notice how the ends of his finger-length russet hair curl just over the collar of his shirt.

Nope. Absolutely not.

Before I do something I probably shouldn't, I head to the bathroom—taking my newly refilled drink with me, because a girl can never be too careful—and a part of me hopes he's gone by the time I return.

Chapter Two

eat a dick

Bentley

I thought I knew how bad jet lag could be, but somehow, I've surpassed the tiredness of my flight from Cusco, Peru to home in Charlotte, North Carolina and entered a state of delirium I've never experienced before.

I try to count the hours it's been since I've properly slept, but all I know is it's nearing two full days. I should have taken some sleeping pills when I got home, but the idea of showing up at my new job sounded better.

That was until I pulled into the parking lot of West-to-East, Inc. and realized what a dick I would look like, dropping in unannounced for my first official visit right as everyone was supposed to be heading home for the day.

So, I left just as quickly as I arrived, but instead of going back home like I should have, I found myself at a local bar I've never been to and hoping for an evening by myself to unwind from my trip. Only, my phone keeps ringing, preventing me from enjoying my hop-heavy beer.

First, it was my sister, making sure I'd made it home and berating me for not checking in with her once I was back at my house.

Now, it's Selene.

I know I shouldn't answer. I know better after our last break-up, but I can't stop my thumb from pressing that green button as her name lights up on my screen. A bad decision that I blame on the jet lag.

"Hello, Bentley," she coos, and the pitch of her voice

is like nails on a chalkboard for me. Another reminder of why I shouldn't have taken the call.

"What do you want, Selene?" I ask with a heavy sigh and feel the creases on my face deepening.

She scoffs with shock. "I miss you, and as soon as Celia told me you were due back today, I couldn't wait any longer to hear your voice."

My fucking sister. Clearly, I need to remind her that *my* business is my own. Not information that needs to be shared with my *ex*-girlfriends.

"Well, I'm busy, so we'll have to chat later," I say and pull the phone away to hang up, but her tone lowers and she calls my name.

"I just... I don't like the way we ended things before you left," she says.

My chuckle turns dark quickly. "You mean you'd like to apologize for saying that my volunteering to help better the communities in third-world countries was a waste of my time since it didn't further my standing within our circles?"

She makes a noise that sounds like she's trying to force herself to cry.

"I *am* sorry, Benny. I didn't mean any of what I said. I just want you back. We belong together. I feel that in my soul."

The way she calls me "Benny" makes me want to stab myself in the eye. The rest of what she has to say used to work on me every time we broke up, but not anymore.

I've seen her true colors a few too many times and I won't go back to that life. Not ever again.

"Nothing has changed, Selene. We broke up for the final time, and we're not getting back together just because I'm home and you've apologized."

She huffs, and all sounds of sadness are gone from her tone. "We're not over, Bentley. I won't accept that."

Then, she hangs up. On me. That woman really is a piece of work.

When my sister introduced us, I thought Selene was a nice person. She played her part almost too well, always talking about how much she loved her family, and how work was something that gave her a purpose, and about the kids she wanted to have because growing up an only child had been torturous for her.

Then, as the months passed and I got to see other sides of her, I realized she is just like my mother. Selene is only looking for a retirement plan in a husband. She wants to be pampered and taken care of. She has no interest in making a difference in the world with our resources.

That woman is everything I never wanted to be after the way I grew up.

Outsiders always look at the rich and think they have it so easy, but growing up with parents who only cared about their bank accounts wasn't anything I wish to repeat for my own life.

For a short time, I thought Selene felt the same way I

did about the way we grew up, but after breaking up and getting back together a couple of times, I've finally realized what we were doing was the definition of insanity. We want very different things out of life, and nothing is ever going to work between us, no matter how much time apart we have.

Fuck. My mood has soured, and I have to piss. I toss a hundred to the bartender who gasps, then I walk off.

I take care of business in the bathroom and exit just in time for the redhead I'd seen earlier to run right into me. Cool, sticky liquid splashes over the front of my new suit, and I step back, pulling the ruined fabric away from my skin.

Her hazel eyes roam over my now see-through dress shirt and she hums. "Well, hello."

"Watch where you're going," I snap.

The flush on her fair cheeks darkens. "Excuse me? You ran into me."

I bark out a deep laugh. "Right, because you were headed toward the men's bathroom to do what exactly?"

It's the only door left down this hallway. She's too drunk to even know which way she was supposed to be going.

"No, I was...looking for a quiet corner...to make a call," she says, her voice lacking the confidence to convince me her words are the truth.

"Right. Well, thanks for ruining my suit." Then, I rake my eyes over her simple green sweater, light jeans with holes in them that are supposed to be fashionable, and back up to her face before shaking my head.

The action isn't necessary, but I'm already annoyed, and she only made things worse by running into me.

I try to brush past her, but she grabs on to my arm, then gestures up and down my body with her other hand. There's fire in her hazel eyes, and her jaw tightens while she stares daggers in my direction.

"Just because you're a rich prick, that doesn't give you the right to look down on me."

I move forward, stepping closer until our faces are only inches apart. "You don't know anything about me."

Her chest expands, and she squares her soft shoulders. "Your five-thousand-dollar suit tells me enough."

"Try *ten* thousand," I goad for no good reason.

Damn, she smells like strawberries and honey.

She shoves me back, sobering by the seconds that I continue to piss her off. "Go back to Madison Park and eat a dick." She turns, then mutters, "And to think I wanted to take him home."

I know she's talking to herself, but I don't miss the disappointment in her quiet tone.

I reach for her wrist and spin her back around. I don't know what I'm doing. I shouldn't touch her. I should let her walk away, but fuck, I suddenly don't want to. Another thing I can blame on the jet lag. Later.

She sucks in a breath, and I pin her against the wall. "How about *I* take *you* home?"

Instead of answering me, she grabs the sides of my face roughly and jerks my head down. Her tongue demands entry into my mouth, and my already-hardening dick stiffens to full mast while she searches every corner of my mouth.

I press my hips against her, and the moan that slips from her mouth is fuel to the sudden inferno inside my body.

My hands tangle with hers, and I drag her from the dark hallway. Unless she has any objections to getting in my car, then I'm about to fuck the snark right out of this fiery woman.

———

Read the rest of A Mutually Beneficial Mistake today on Amazon and Kindle Unlimited!

Printed in Great Britain
by Amazon